San Andreas Island

By Angela Costello

LAMindSpa Publishing LLC

Published in the United States of America in 2019 by
LAMindSpa Publishing LLC
Copyright © Angela Costello 2019

This novel is a work of fiction. The names, characters,
and incidents portrayed in it are the work of the author's imagination, or moderately inspired by true
events. Any resemblance to actual persons, living or
dead, events or localities, is coincidental - or if moderately inspired by true events, names and characteristics
have been changed to protect their identities.

Printed and bound by KDP
Visit the author at www.LAMindSpa.com

For Sabrina

"The world breaks everyone and afterward many are strong at the broken places."

— Ernest Hemingway

Table of Contents

Chapter One:

Sunkissed Café (Spring 2023)

Ugg. I need air.

I stuff my notebook, along with all my feelings, deep into my work bag and grab my phone. My heart races a bit as I flip through all of his texts again. Why does he have to send these strange messages and creep me out like this? Why can't he just send me something like, "Hi, I miss you." I really don't want to deal with this right now. I text Helen and Sarah and ask if they still plan to meet.

Helen: Don't flake Jelina! I already got a table

Sarah: Order me a Pinot

Me: Walking out now. See you in a few. xo

I grab my wristlet purse and throw in my keys, debit card, and lipgloss. I set the alarm on my phone, giving me enough time to walk there and make it back for my last two patients of the day. I flip the sign on the door from *Jelina King - In Session* to *Jelina King - Out of Office* and head down the narrow hallway to the confidential exit. This exit was the deciding factor when I chose to lease this place two years ago. My patients can leave difficult sessions without facing a waiting room full of people, and savor in the emotional safety. The other three *In Session* signs on the hallway doors inform me that we have a packed house in here right now, but you'd never know it—the only thing I hear are the white noise machines in the hallway.

I unzip my wristlet and triple check that I have my keys. I've locked myself out one too many times before. My hand quietly closes the main door behind me, and I glance up at the open air atrium which our offices encircle. The rainfall from the morning has cleared out. The intense sunlight blinds me for a moment, but there's that fresh air I've been yearning for. I take a long intentional inhale, like a drag from a cigarette, although I've never actually put a cigarette to my lips, so I just imagine it's a similar inhale, and I walk by the planter boxes of sprawling ivy with pops of Cattleya Orchids, go past the elevator, and go down five flights of stairs. I wave hello to the accountant whose office is a fishbowl for everyone who waits by the elevator on the ground floor. I push open the creaky door. I've emailed Maintenance twice already, but I might as well bring in my own WD-40. The gate slams behind me.

Ocean Avenue is bustling with the usual mix of tourists and locals. I'm curious to know what these locals do for a living that they have the luxury of hanging out at the pier in the middle of a Monday. Maybe they're all pot dealers and growers. Maybe they have rich parents and husbands who help with the bills. I cross Washington Avenue and walk by the old guy who's playing guitar. I'm convinced he lives on that corner and probably plays those same songs in his sleep. I wave to see if he'll surprise me today and actually lift his head from underneath his hat. No dice. I shrug. I wonder what his story is. He's comforting and using his talent to help brighten people's day as we all walk by him.

I pass the tourists with cameras around their necks, not using their phones surprisingly, but taking photos of the view from the stoplight. I have to say, even though I walk by here everyday, that view on this palm tree lined street is still nothing less than spectacular. The sky is painted pale blue with splashes of orange and pink. The sunlight hits the water in such a way that I swear, shimmering diamonds are floating on the waves.

A flock of seagulls soars by me. The sounds of their cawing combined with the waves crashing at the shoreline are a symphonic soundtrack to this serene beachfront view. A surfer walks by me holding his board, followed by three college-aged girls riding by on skateboards, wearing bikini tops and cheeky shorts (that I'll never let Lily wear). They leave the scent of suntan lotion in their wake. I reach the corner of Wilshire and Ocean, passing the chic restaurants and five-star hotels I'll never afford as a guest.

Natural stone steps lead me to the café, where I hear what sounds like Italian music. The mix of guitar and piano are playing through speakers tucked near the base of the palm trees. It's a light-hearted melody, with a strong female voice. Wood outdoor wall panels and fresh succulents adorn this hot spot, and create frames around the wide open windows and the guests seated inside. I see a mixed crowd, some wearing the classic entrepreneur-at-a-laptop look, while others appear to be the Instagram models I follow, down to the beachy wave hair, strappy sandals and rib-cage tattoos. One of them is Sarah. I spot her and Helen at a table near the koi pond.

Helen works for one of the most vile attorneys in Los Angeles. She's classy as usual this afternoon in a cream silk blouse, pinstripe slacks and black pumps. Her strawberry blonde waves are never out of place, and today they're pinned up on the right: a nice Marilyn Monroe look.

Sarah runs a discreet psychic reading business for elite professionals in Beverly Hills. Today, she's wearing a small French braid on one side and her dark brown waves have a chunk of blue peeking from underneath. Her jeans are ripped at the thighs, and her blue tank is hugging her thin frame. I look down at my plain top as I make my way towards them and touch my newly trimmed hair. How are they even friends with me?

As I approach the table, I can hear them mid-conversation around their favorite obsession: how to find the right guy.

"Hi ladies," I say, leaning over as we exchange cheek kisses.

"I like this much better," Sarah says as she touches the tips of my hair.

"You might as well have gone shorter, but I like it," Helen winks at me.

They've already dipped into their wine. I see a small cheese platter on the table with Brie, Gouda, goat cheese, grapes, nuts and fig spread. The waitress greets me with a hot ginger tea and honey on the side.

"You two take care of me better than anyone," I say, stirring the honey stick inside the teacup, taking a sip and setting it aside to cool. They start picking at various cheeses, and I grab a few grapes.

Sarah looks over at Helen, "Ok, this is what you should put."

Helen hands her phone over. "Here, I trust you ladies with my life."

Sarah reads what she's typing aloud. "I enjoy creating memories that make my heart beat faster, books that make me feel like I'm in another world for a bit, movies that make me think about life differently, and making new friends. I like to wake up when my body is ready, run outside in the mornings a couple times a week when the city is still quiet, buy too many books, check out a new restaurant, and walk to the beach when I have a long break at work or on weekends."

Helen responds, "I'm not *that* Plain Jane. It's missing 'you better know how to make me scream'."

My tea shoots out my nose, and I'm simultaneously laughing and coughing.

Sarah gives Helen her phone back, takes a sip of her Pinot and says, "You have no idea. Believe it or not, guys are more sensitive than us. They get so needy and want to cuddle. You have to think about that when you're on these apps. I saw that 24-year-old again last night—"

I interrupt her. "Sarah, he's 24? You never told me that. Oh my God. That's like ten years! Too young."

"Too hot," she says with a grin.

Helen encourages her. "That sounds kinda fun, actually." She swirls her wine and takes a sip.

"You're both weird. Ok, go on," I say.

Sarah leans in. "So he gets to my place, and I don't want to deal with any romantic b.s. right? I answer the door in my black lace teddy and stilettos, grab his shirt and pull him towards me and start slowly kissing his neck and then his mouth. Right there, in the doorway. I honestly couldn't care less if my neighbors walked by. And he was such a good kisser. He's 6'4"! So tall that he had to lean over so I could reach him! I stopped and took his hand and led him to my room. He rocked my world. I swear."

Helen can't help herself. "Damn, girl."

"I miss that so much," I say. For now, I settle on savoring each sip of my tea and our bites of cheese, and being here right now with these two.

"Yeah, well, it was exactly what I needed. Except for the fact that it took a lot of repeating that he had to wear protection," Sarah says. "I don't get why these guys whine so much about it. Anyway, it was hot, but then he got all sensitive, and didn't want to leave. After we both came, I was good. He was cleaning himself up in the bathroom and throwing out the condom, and I had already folded his clothes and was getting him a bottle of water for the road from the kitchen. He came out in his boxer briefs—he looked like a Calvin Klein model, and he was half laughing and like, 'Are you kicking me out? You don't want to lay down and hang out for a while?' And I told him I had a great time, and he was amazing, but I was going to sleep early and had an important meeting for work in the morning. He looked at me like a sad little puppy. I felt so bad, but I really don't have time for feelings and all that in my life right now."

"Oh my God, you're unreal," I say, with a laugh.

"So anyway, he got dressed, kissed me and hugged me for an awkward minute. Then I thanked him for coming and walked him to the door."

"Wow, that's harsh," Helen says.

"I would settle for that any day," I say, finishing the last of my tea. "I still can't believe these dat-

13

ing apps exist. Too many options, and people always think the grass is greener and it's just a swipe away. It's like sitting at a slot machine, when you're supposed to get up after a good win."

"Hey, it's worth the gamble, isn't it?" Sarah says.

The waitress comes by and replaces my tea kettle with ginger shots. "Need anything else, ladies?"

"I'll have another Pinot!" Sarah announces. I raise my eyebrows. "What?" She snaps at me. "We only live once, honey."

The waitress gives her a thumbs-up and vanishes.

I wince as I down my ginger shot. I forgot to ask for a chaser. "What I don't get is, how do all these people do it? Really. Work, take care of a child, take care of a husband, come home, cook, clean, laundry, bath times." I tuck my hair behind my ear. "It's literally impossible."

Helen has the same look on her face she had when she told me her grandmother was sick. "You look exhausted, J, all the time. I mean, for some crazy reason, you're trying to be Superwoman, and I hate to break it to you, but you're not. You're human like the rest of us. Except you're so busy trying to be perfect, you're disappearing. We can't even get you to come out with us and have a proper drink."

My phone alarm chimes, and that's my cue to escape this anxiety ridden spotlight. Thank God.

"It's been fun ladies, but I have to go. Let me know how much I owe you," I say, standing up and leaning over to give kisses on cheeks.

I put my Superwoman cape back on.

Chapter Two:

Pitch Black

Why is it pitch black in here? I swear I left the hallway light on last night in case Lily woke up. There isn't a single car on the road outside our window, so I'm guessing it's about two a.m.

-Click-

Ok, that sound is definitely coming from the front of the house—the kitchen, maybe? My body stiffens and presses itself deeper into the mattress. I switch on the lamp sitting on the nightstand. I look over at the perfectly made half of the bed next to me. He's still not back, and I didn't hear the garage door. He never enters from the front of the house, unless he's walking in from hanging out at the beach. After

35 years on this planet, I would think freaking out over noises at night would be a thing of the past. This is one of those moments why I like sleeping with someone: you know, for backup to fight the bad guys.

-Click-

There it is again! Despite the air conditioner being set at a cool 68 degrees, my brain sends streams of sweat to my palms, shifting this situation from a *Category 1: It's Nothing*, up to a *Category 4: Now I Really Have To Get Up*. I roll my eyes to no audience when I realize I left my iPhone at the office, and of course this is the one time I would need a landline. If anything happens, I'll scream and my hot neighbor across the street will rescue me well before the police would arrive anyway.

I stretch my arm out over the side of the bed and reach underneath the box spring. My hand tap-dances around until it lands on the flashlight, then my slippers. It's not satisfied. It keeps dancing for a bit and stops when it feels the long cloth case it's been searching for. With the case squeezed between my fingertips, I roll back over and onto my pillow. I lift the flap and grab the smooth, strong handle of the most dangerous object I own (one that's been laying there patiently for this kind of action all year): my old cooking knife. I put it aside for a moment, sit up and pull my hair into a high ponytail. I'm still adjusting to this length, although I agree with Helen and wish I'd gone a bit shorter. I grab my weapon. Armed and ready, here we go.

The cool breeze from the air vent tingles my partly opened lips, glides over my tongue and drains into my lungs. "Relax, Jelina," I say aloud. The surge of electricity passes through my chest, across my arms and makes its way into my fingertips. My eyes and mind are fixated on every muscle and bone in my feet, attempting to transform them into quiet feathers as they make their way across each hardwood plank in this hallway and towards the front of the house. Clutching my knife with my dominant hand, I pass Lily's room, and my left hand presses a gentle high five on her door. The peaceful dreamer assures me she's ok with her soft snores. I pull her doorknob towards me to triple-check that she is safe and secure in there, release my grip and continue on my mission. I look down at my feathers. They've stayed silent as I continue to creep through the hallway. I'm as close to the wall as I can get without letting my skin touch it. I perfected this skill when Lily was a baby, since studying the quiet spots meant sleep and sanity for all.

I peek around the corner. My heart sounds like someone's playing drumsticks in all four chambers. My eyes search the darkness for whatever forced me out of that cozy bed. Nothing. The hum of the air conditioner fills the room. And my God, whose idea was it to cook salmon earlier? The stench is distracting and seeping into my pores. After what feels like an eternity, my feathers carry me right here, underneath the entryway of the kitchen.

My fingers are tempted to switch the light on, but I command them to stop. My heart is beating out of my chest.

I'm straining my eyes to try to make out what that glowing object is on the kitchen floor, but it seems like someone's filled the room with fog.

As I inch my way closer, I learn that the blurry thing in front of me is in fact a sweet little blonde girl. My heart feels warm with ease being in her presence and catches a normal rhythm. I lower my knife so as to not frighten her.

Her stick-straight golden hair is tied back and she's sitting cross-legged. Her big brown eyes don't even look up at me; they're glued to the notebook she has resting in her lap. She's writing something in it.

-Click-

My head jerks in the direction of that sound across the room, to the front door. My arm obeys my anxiety's orders and returns the knife to its protective position. That click is coming from the other side of the front door. Ever so still, with knife in hand, I step across the smooth kitchen tile, and a shiver runs down my spine. I can't tell if that's from panic or if the air is on too low for this Cali native. In pin-drop silence, I get on my tiptoes and extend my neck towards the peephole, but immediately retract it back into my shell. What if the mysterious bad guy can see a change in light from the other side of the peephole, or any sign that I'm here? *Jelina, they engineer these things for a reason*, I think to myself. I surrender, hold my breath, and let my gaze fall into the tiny looking glass. There's a gun pointed in my direction, but there's a phone in the other hand, snapping pictures and waiting to stalk my every move.

-Click -

My hands are dripping with sweat, and my panic turns into nausea when I see who it is.

Chapter Three:

Lilykin

"Mommy. Mommmyyy."

My eyes peel open, and through their blurry slits, I see the inviting amber dawn from my bedroom window.   "Oh, thank God," I whisper, as my breath hugs my lungs. I let my eyelids rest again and a deep exhale pushes past my lips. It felt so real this time. On autopilot, my arm extends to learn what time it is, and stretches towards the nightstand to where my phone typically beckons me. A subtle wave of phone withdrawal and irritation hits me when I remember my phone hasn't miraculously transported here from my office.

"Mommmyyy."

My body follows its usual routine in response to this command: with my eyes still closed, I roll to the side and push off the bed with my left hand. "Ow!" I look down. The tip of my cooking knife is pricking the palm of my hand. Ugh, this sleepwalking is getting really old.

"Mommmyyy." Lily tries one last time to summon me from her room down the hall. Her sweet voice shakes me out of this bizarre reality test. I wince at the dime-sized spot of blood on my hand, and wipe it on my pajamas. I lean over the side of the bed and toss the knife to its original home.

My sleepy-eyed four-year-old alarm clock walks into the room. It's the strangest feeling to have my body annoyed about being woken up at a ridiculous hour, but for all that annoyance to melt away when I see her. My hips hinge my upper body back onto the bed. I can feel my face soften as I see Lily's blonde curls bouncing. She clutches her favorite monkey, Max, in one hand, and her blanket in the other. This blanket was the smoothest fleece that Dylan and I could find when she was a baby. It's been through hundreds of laundry cycles since. Max is still intact; his lanky arms and legs swing from side to side as Lily closes the gap between us.

We flow into the unspoken mini ritual we've created together every time Dylan goes out. Our mouths don't utter a word, but our eyes say, "Let's snuggle." She's tall enough now to climb onto my bed without help. We've done this dance dozens of times, and each and every time, she snuggles into me, closes her eyes, and I hold her close and wish that I could magically keep her this safe in my arms forever. I can only see her profile as Lily's cheeks puff up with her smile. Her long dark eyelashes tell me her eyes are opening. She turns her head and then her body, never letting go of her blanket and Max, as if they're stuck to her hands. Her face shines with her bright smile and her eyes meet mine. She nuzzles into me even closer. This is home.

Lily's little arm moves next to mine, and she looks at our matching birthmarks. Her hand grabs mine and guides it to her face. I follow her nonverbal request. I let my index finger gently trace her eyebrows, then down the bridge of her nose, around her cupid's bow lips, drawing the outline of her face starting from her chin up to her soft cheeks and across her forehead. She's simply perfect.

My heart starts to feel heavy, and my chest stings a little. This is how it's supposed to be, right here in this moment: tender, sweet, calm—no fear, no chaos. She reminds me so much of myself when I was her age: attached to my mom's leg in public, always looking down and not daring to lock eyes with anyone. I would have diagnosed myself with Selective Mutism when I was four, and Lily seems to be the same. You're lucky if she says a word to you if you're not family, and she has the same permanent frown on her face that I did when anyone talks to her. A tear escapes my eye, and I raise my shoulder towards my cheek to wipe it dry. My tracing finger is resting on Lily's temple. "Again, Mommy," she whispers as she falls asleep.

The clank from the garage door jolts me out of this bliss. Dylan's home. Late, of course, but home. I look over at Lily. She's sound asleep.

Not only does he drain our accounts with nights like this, but he just never listens. I wish he would take an Uber like I tell him to when he goes out, or not get obliterated every time he's with friends, but he insists that he sobers up with water at the end of the night. Fine, I'll never win any of our arguments. I just hope he doesn't reek of liquor.

The sunlight bleeds through the blinds and spills onto the bed, alerting me that it's shower time. I climb over Lily and let her sleep for a bit longer.

I meet Dylan at the bathroom door and he shuffles towards me. A wave of irritation rises in my stomach as I breathe in the whiskey he swore he wouldn't drink last night. I push down all my feelings and put on my Super-wife cape.

"Hi honey," I manage, pecking him with an obligatory kiss. My closed lips force a smile. Isn't this what a good wife is supposed to do?

His bloodshot eyes are too tired to maintain contact. "Hey babe," he says, and he pushes past me, making it just in time to get to the toilet and not vomit on the floor. The pungent odors of his fun night fill the room. My stomach and esophagus dry heave as my body fights the reflex to put my own head in the toilet. I can't believe this is happening again! I let myself sink into the most familiar role I know: caretaker. My open hand lays against his slouched back, massaging and soothing him in a circular motion.

I'm reminded of the nightmare last night when my palm stings, and I push the image of that face from behind the door out of my mind.

I look up and catch a glimpse of Dylan's eyes from his profile. I can see a hint of the man I married. There he is.

These moments drive me crazy. They're so back and forth between love and hate. This isn't really him. I glance over at Lily, whose eyes are fluttering open.

"Hun, I'm gonna shower and then get Lily ready for school. Next time, can you promise to take an Uber?" Even as the words leave my mouth, I know I'm wasting my breath. He peels his body away from the toilet and drags himself to the sink. My Dylan is starting to come back as he splashes water on his face and swishes a capful of mouthwash.

I flush the toilet for him, wash my hands, and find myself behind him. Both of my hands reach up to massage his shoulders, and run my fingers through his sandy blonde hair and let my thumb and fingertips massage his neck. I can't remember the last time we had sex. Feeling his skin against mine right now makes me yearn for more. I press my lips against the spot between his shoulder blades. He rotates his entire body on his left foot, looks at me with his heart-stopping emerald eyes. He wraps his arms around my waist, then brings one hand up to play with my hair.

"I thought you weren't going to cut it," he furrows his brow.

"I only took off a few inches. It's still long," I feel the sting of shame, being inspected and not good enough. "I like it," I say softly, my pathetic attempt at asserting myself.

"Ok," he huffs, kisses me on the forehead - kissing away any erotic craving I just had.

"Ewwwww," Lily says through giggles. She's gotten herself out of bed and is barreling towards us. She stretches out her hands, jumps up and wraps her arms and legs around our thighs like a little cub. My muscles tighten in an effort to not lose my balance. This must be all the energy she holds in when she's walking around shy and quiet all day outside of these four walls. Lily leans her torso back, keeping a good grip on us, looks at Dylan, points to her nose and sings, "Daddyyyy!"

Dylan picks her up high in the air and kisses her on the nose, "Myy liiittle Liilykin," he says in a singsong tone.

"Lily *King,* Daddy," she giggles as he puts her back down. Their exchange is one of my favorite things to watch.

"I'm hungry!" Lily announces.

"Babe," Dylan's eyes beg me to rescue him.

"I got it, hun," I say and kiss him on the lips, grateful he used mouthwash.

"I'm gonna lay down for a bit," he says, taking off his shoes and his clothes. He puts on his pajamas and climbs into bed. I can't help but roll my eyes. Am I jealous or angry?

I squat down in front of Lily and sweep strands of hair away from her face, tucking them behind her ear.

"Daddy's going to rest and I'll make some oatmeal for you after we get ready, ok?"

Lily bounces back to her room, and I shift into overdrive.

Dylan left his phone in the bathroom. I check the time. I have exactly 42 minutes until we need to be in the car and heading to school.

In one swift move, my fingertips turn the shower knob all the way to the left and I wait until the water gets warm. I swivel around to face the glass bowl sink and lean over and brush my teeth. The steam from the shower paints a thin layer of fog on the mirror. I catch my reflection before it's fully effaced, and gasp for a second when I see that face from my nightmare and he's standing behind me! I flip around and there's no one there. Ugggg! I don't have time for this! I flip back around and cup water into my hands and rinse out my mouth, clean my toothbrush, tap it on the edge of the sink and toss it into its holder.

My vision clears again, and my mind returns back here in this bathroom. I fixate on the freestanding vessel bowl we had installed last year. I follow the ice-blue lines that were designed with an artistic hand to look like soft waves on the beach—you know how they layer and rest near the sand? I let my fingers play with the warm water flowing from the waterfall faucet. I turn my head to the right, looking at the real waves outside my window in the distance. It's so beautiful and peaceful out there. The palm trees, the flowers, the endless ocean; it's an unreachable world.

I pull my attention back inside and shut off the water. As much as I try to resist looking in the mirror, my eyes rebel. I see that my reflection is just a shell of a woman who's becoming more and more invisible each day. I've lost my identity. I'm looking at a stranger. What's wrong with me? When did this happen? I raise my hand to my cheek and feel my skin. I'm disappearing. My already thin frame is melting away. I'm such a zombie. I look in the mirror at those dark circles, those same eyes that were once smiling and now hollow and empty. Marriage has made me invisible—dead.

I'm struck by the photo of Dylan and me, hanging on the wall in a green frame. It's strange how the younger versions of ourselves are preserved in blurry old photos. I think we'd only been dating for a few months when that was taken. We were on vacation in Maldives and celebrating my birthday. We looked attractive and so young and in love. I feel tears trickling down my cheeks. My vision is getting distorted now, but I focus on the green frame. I'm dissociating, traveling back and forth from that trip all those years ago when life was actually fun and then coming back to the chaos that has now become my life, crying myself to sleep more times than I'd care to admit. Where did those lovebirds go? Did they die? Are they just buried under a huge pile of distraction, waiting to be uncovered? Was that love even real? It had to be. It's still there. I feel it. I want us back. I miss my Dylan.

I pull the faucet lever towards me on the sink so that the mini waterfall streams down. I cup the water in my hands and rinse out my mouth, and then splash water onto my face, feeling the instant soothing sensation on my burning bloodshot eyes. I push the faucet lever back, and the waterfall goes away. I grab a hand towel and pat my skin dry. I glance again at that photo of the couple who no longer exists. I see her eyes and his, and they're smiling—really smiling. They were a happy couple. The one everyone compared themselves to. They were in love; deeply in love. And love goes through deaths and births. We just need something to come in and revive us.

The bright numbers on Dylan's phone smack me in the face with reality. 33 minutes left. I slip off my pajamas and hop into the shower, that's been running the entire time I drifted into la-la land. *Nice, J. You just wasted a bathtub full of water.* It's almost burning my skin. Trying to beat the clock, I don't stray from my routine: wash my face, shampoo and condition my hair. I feel as if I'm standing across from myself, watching as I'm shaving my legs. I'm looking down at my body in a way I would imagine seeing myself through someone else's eyes. A wave of sadness comes over me.

"Mommy!" Lily calls from her room. "I can't find my funny sweater," she says, or so I think, because the sounds of the shower muffle her words.

"Just a minute!" I say loudly. *Her funny sweater?*

"What?!" she yells.

"Lily, can you come here, please? I've told you I can't hear you when I'm in the shower." I'm almost done mowing the lawn on my legs, and I nick the same spot on my knee every time. The water tries to hide the blood that's now confidently leaking out of that razor slice, as I'm pushing away the images that flash in my mind from that nightmare: that haunting face stalking me, having this power over me. I lather my body with soap, and wish I could tell the water to move faster across my skin.

My first mission is completed in what I think is a new record time. The volume lowers to mute in this tiny room when I move the shower lever all the way to *Off*. I close my eyes and sneak in a 20-second spa vacation. The steam cleanses my pores, and keeps me goosebump-free as I'm dripping wet.

Lily peeks her head between the shower curtain and the wall, adorable and annoyed. "Mommy, I said I can't find my bunny sweater. The one I got from Grandma and Grandpa."

Ah, her *bunny* sweater. I grab my towel and point to the bedroom. "I did laundry last night, sweetie. It's folded in the stack of clothes on top of my dresser."

"Oh!" she peeps and disappears. I wipe most of my body down, let what's left air dry, bend over so that my hair is dangling downward, and wrap it in my towel. I flip back up and catch a glimpse of myself in the mirror. My collarbone is sticking out. That new; can't be good.

Dylan's phone vibrates with a notification, snapping me out of this hard look at reality. I swipe my thumb upwards to clear his recurring "Gym at 8 AM" reminder.

"Ha," an annoyed laugh escapes my lips.

I have 23 minutes before we need to be out the door. I fall back onto the racetrack that is my life. Deodorant, foundation, mascara, lip gloss. I'm like a robot. Serve people, work, serve people, work. I guess this is the life I signed up for.

I loosen the towel and hang it on the rack, let my hair fall down and back, and brush out the tangles. I fly into the bedroom and land in my closet. My hand doesn't have the patience to figure out what to wear today, and just snags the usual. I slide on my bra and panties, throw on black slacks and gray top, being careful not to wake Dylan. Who am I kidding? He wouldn't move an inch if Lily and I started jumping on the bed. He should be helping me anyway. I look up and see my old books and college spiral bound notebooks tucked in the corner on the shelf of the closet. I let my fingers grab the only notebook that still gets attention these days. and pull it out. I sit down on the carpet in this small space, with my back against the hanging jackets, and flip through the handwritten pages.

March 15, 2015

I'm in a fairytale. I swear! He bumped into me today near the psych building, right after Professor Burgeon's class. I practically died when he started talking to me. He said he's majoring in law, which is amazing. He's seriously the hottest guy on campus. My heart was beating so fast, I thought it was going to fly right out of my chest and land on the ground between us. He looked like he walked straight out of a photo shoot. His sandy blonde hair was messy, but in that perfect hot guy kind of messy. And he stood there in front of me so tall, without a care in the world. And his eyes, oh my God I was entranced by his emerald eyes. I was in bliss for a good minute and a half. There were actual sparkling flecks in his eyes!

I flip some pages.

September 3, 2015

Oh my God!!!! I can't believe what just happened!! Dylan said we were just going over to his parents' house for dinner. They've been over our place a couple of times, but I was kinda nervous about finally going to their house. And Oh. My. God. His father is an architect and designed most of the properties n Malibu sitting along PCH, including their own house. We pulled up to the gate, and I had to pick my jaw up off the floor when I realized his home looks like the Four Seasons. I knew they had money, but wow. Their mansion sprawls across a few acres of land, which is rare

*for LA. After the housekeeper buzzed us in, we drove
along the palm tree-lined road, past Charlie and
Winifred, their horses?? past the tennis court!? past
the fruit trees, an organic vegetable garden. It's out of
this world. We had the windows down and it was
amazing! The drive up to their house is filled with
scents of orange, lemon, fig... We get inside their
12,000-square-foot Malibu pad, that has an elevator?!
floor-to-ceiling glass doors that overlook an infinity
pool with ocean views, and a wraparound deck with a
fire pit. The chef and housekeeper's quarters are in the
back, which is triple the size of my family's Valencia
apartment. Dylan blindfolded me and I was so weirded
out. Why is he doing one of his surprise things now??
I started getting annoyed at him and said I don't want
my eye makeup to get messed up with his little games,
and want tonight to be special. He secured the blindfold even tighter and took my hand as he walked me
through the house and out to the backyard. Oh my
god!! He takes the blindfold off and I'm standing in
the middle of their enormous beautifully lit garden,
surrounded by his parents and his sister, AND my mom
and Kyle were even there! Seeing my brother had me
instantly know something was up. Sarah and Helen
were there! Jake and Jane. Everyone knew! And then
the most incredible thing ever happened! I still can't*

believe it. Just like in the movies. Dylan got down on one knee and asked me to marry him! I started crying and couldn't even believe what was happening, that I didn't even respond. And of course I ended up saying yes! Then he put this huge diamond on my finger. I've never even had a diamond anything in my life. Oh my God I'm getting married!!

I flip some more.

September 20, 2016–

My trip down memory lane gets interrupted by a loud thunk comes from down the hall. *"I'm ok!"* Lily's voice calls out, reassuring me. She knows my *Mom Worry Reaction* all too well by now.

"Ok!" I shout back. I snap the notebook shut and toss it into my work bag. I tuck my top into my pants, and blindly grab the first pair of flats my hands find. I check on Lily's status. I can see her at the end of the hallway, sitting at her desk, writing. She's wearing her bunny sweater—and *only* her bunny sweater!

"Lily!? Oh my God! Put your pants on! We have to go!" I can't believe I'm yelling at her. I've been lagging as much as she has. I look over at Dylan. His snores are an obnoxious confirmation of the hier-

archy in this marriage. My organs are on fire and my blood is filled with rage.

Chapter Four:

What Crazy Feels Like

As luck would have it, my umbrella is still right where I left it the last time it rained—in the trunk of the car. I somehow manage to make Lily oatmeal on the go, and get us out of the house on time. I grab my jacket and use it to cover her and her backpack as we run out to the car. The rain is coming down and dampening my hair, my clothes, and my work bag in the 40 seconds it's taking me to get from the front door to my car. None of us Angelenos were prepared for this bizarre June rainfall. But here we are.

We buckle ourselves in when we get into the car and I look in the rear view mirror and see that Lily's buckled, too. I pull out of the driveway. The thought of Dylan sleeping in our warm bed while I'm out here just gets under my skin. I hate him right now.

Why does he get to park in the garage? Why does he get to have the cushy life? Wouldn't it be nice if I could quit every time I didn't care for a job? He knows I won't quit mine. Why do I have to suffer the consequences of his hangovers? He doesn't even care about respecting me anymore. I chose to get married, so these are the cards I've been dealt.

I see Lily in my rear-view mirror, scooping her oatmeal and looking out the window. She's a warm summer breeze amidst my internal chaos.

"What do you see out there?" I ask her.

"The Magic Sand Castle House," she continues to stare out the window.

I look in the direction of where she's looking, and I remember the one she's talking about. We pass it when we go on walks in the neighborhood. She's right. It does actually look like a magic sand castle with its shape and that shiny silver door.

"I don't want anymore," she says, handing me almost a full cup of oatmeal. Before I can grab it, I feel it hit the back of my elbow and spill all over the floor mat and her shoes.

"*God*!" I shout. Lily looks at me with shame.

"It's ok," I manage to let out - but we both know how I really feel.

I stuff my anger, just as I find a parking spot—
further away than I'd like, but at least I found one. I
look back at the spilled oatmeal and roll my eyes as I
park the car. I feel like a horrible mom for being upset
at her for an innocent mistake. I'm not even going to
deal with cleaning that up right now. She unbuckles
herself from the booster seat while I grab the umbrella
and step out of the car. She pulls her backpack on over
her shoulders, climbs out of the car and we share the
umbrella as we rush to school. The same moms I see
every morning are waiting at the gate, and their looks
of judgment pierce me with shame behind their "Good
Morning's" and A-framed hugs. I wish my face wasn't
so transparent, but no one could put enough cucum-
bers on my eyes to hide the fact that I haven't felt rested in years.

"Are you ok? You look a little tired," the tall
one asks, more as an announcement to everyone that
I'm not ok, rather than genuine human concern. I hate
that she just said that, and I never understand why
people do. You might as well tell me I look ugly as
hell. And do you really think I'm going to tell you how
I am right here, right now, standing in this spotlight at
school?   I feel a lump in my throat, my palms are
sweating and the nausea and stinging in my chest tug
at me, pulling me into a silent panic attack from social

anxiety. I think I can hide this one if my throat doesn't close up and I don't start hyperventilating.

"I'm fine," I say with a fake smile. *FINE: F'd up, Insecure, Neurotic, Emotional.* I'm holding Lily, and grateful for the rain so I can hide under the umbrella.

It takes every ounce of energy I have to stay standing here for Lily until the bell rings. I thought we were late, and now I kind of wish we were so we don't have to tolerate this any longer. The bell finally saves us, announcing that this high school clique flashback is over. I kiss and hug Lily goodbye, but she holds me tightly and her eyes look so sad and scared, desperate for me not to leave. The teachers have told me it's really hard for her to make friends because she's so shy at school and it looks like she's mad because she frowns all the time, and doesn't want to play or talk to the other children. She only wants to sit with Miss Kayla who braids her hair and sings her songs. I don't know if she's ever going to be rid of her separation anxiety. I see Miss Kayla walking towards the gate, and I'm relieved. I need to get to work and out of my shame spiral. She squats down to Lily's eye level and speaks gently.

"Good morning, my little butterfly," Miss Kayla says to Lily, who doesn't detach from my leg, but manages to meet her eyes—barely. Lily's told me at home that she thinks it's "so funny" when Miss Kayla calls the kids butterflies. You'd never know it from looking at her right this second.

"I got some new cocoons for our classroom, and there's a very special red butterfly that hatched last night. C'mon, I want to show you."

"A red one?" Lily's curiosity breaks down her wall.

"Yes," Miss Kayla says. "They're little visitors from up there." She points to the sky, and then reaches out her hand. I kiss the top of Lily's head as she releases my leg and she gives me a look that reads, *Who on earth would decline a butterfly invitation?*

The rain has stopped. I pull my umbrella closed. I'm rushing to get back to my car, and all these parents are blocking my path! Literally standing in the middle of the sidewalk chatting like it's a Saturday afternoon. I'm for sure going to be late.

I picture Dylan still sleeping, or in his pajamas lounging on the couch, relaxed as can be. God! Why can't he help me in the mornings and drop her off? Why can't he get up and help me with her breakfast, or get her ready for school? Why does he have an excuse for everything? Why can't he see how stressed I am, doing it all on my own? Does he even notice or care?

I find myself standing in front of my car, all the way down the street. I'm fumbling with my keys to get inside, and when I do, my body drops into the seat, letting the door slam shut. The smell of oatmeal and musty rain seep into my pores. My body fills up with rage and the next thing I know, I'm hitting the steering wheel, spilling out all my anger, resentment, sadness and hurt onto it. My hands slam against it, and then I clench my fists, banging them against my legs. I hate him! I hate him! I'm trapped!

The backs of my forearms hit my thighs. "*God! This is too hard! I can't do this anymore!*" I'm sobbing and yelling at the top of my lungs so forcefully for what feels like forever, that I'm losing my voice. I don't even bother to wipe the tears away, because they continue to pour down my cheeks. My eyes are swollen and hurting. The tops of my thighs are throbbing. I shake out of my momentary rage spiral and start to panic, remembering where I am. I push my sleeves up and check my forearms. My heart sinks for a moment, then shifts to panic when I see the evidence of my "crazy." This pain will turn into bruises tomorrow. I'll have to remember to wear long sleeves again to avoid interrogations from my colleagues. *What happened to your arms? Did someone do this to you?* No, it's just me and my rage. It's no big deal. I can't hit anyone or punch a wall, so this is where my anger goes.

I'm barely able to keep my hand steady enough to get the key in the ignition. This is what crazy feels like. Right here. He drives me out of my mind!

And I have no right to complain. So many people have it way worse than this. The silence in this car wraps me up like a warm blanket. I've landed in the only place in the entire world where I can mute the chaos.

I start the engine and take a deep breath. I can't believe I just lost it like this. I would die if anyone saw me.

My cell phone vibrates and the call connects my mom automatically through the car speakers. She insists on calling me every morning on my drive to work. I've been avoiding her and Kyle, not answering their calls or texts, because I don't want to be a burden and have them listen to my complaints or ask if I'm ok. I'm not ok, but I'm really trying. I swear, I'm trying with all my might to be positive. I show up to work every single day, I care about every single one of my patients, and I've applied to adjunct teaching jobs to see if I can make some extra money. But I've made my world so small. I'm trying with every ounce of energy I have to put one foot in front of the other and survive this life I've found myself in. It's so hard to stop crying, though. Ugh.

"Hi, Mom!" I force a cheery voice. I can't have her worrying about me right now. I just can't.

"Good morning, sweetheart. How are you?" she asks. Good, she hasn't noticed. She's never not in a good mood.

"I'm fine," I force the words out.

"You're not ok. I can hear it in your voice. And Kyle told me he hasn't heard from you for a while. What's wrong?" she persists. She's right. I haven't talked to my brother in weeks.

"I'm fine, Mom. Just tired," I lie. *Please talk to me about work or Kyle or anything else.*

"You've been crying. Tell me, honey. What happened?" Her words are now intense and her tone went from worried to panic. How can moms tell and why do they have to go straight to panic? It just stresses us out even more.

"Ugh, it's just...I don't know. Everything?!" My tears have their own agenda and there's no stopping them now. I don't know if they'll ever end. I turn off the engine. I can't drive like this. I can't even see straight.

"It's so hard to be a mom, and a wife and just everything. And I'm so angry all the time. I can't stop my panic attacks, and I think I was sleepwalking again. I just can't keep it together and I can't stop crying! Like right now. I don't know what's wrong with me. Is this what depression feels like? All this anger pressing down inside of me?"

I continue my rant. "And people keep asking me at work if I'm ok, and I have no idea how to answer them because I have no idea why I'm such a mess! I should be happy and grateful. I have Lily and Dylan, and we have our beautiful house and I have my clients. I shouldn't be complaining. So many people in this world have it so much worse." I'm already exhausted from this conversation. And I know what's waiting for me later is an emotional hangover.

"Honey, slow down. It's going to be ok, I promise you." She's trying. She really is.

"Mom--" I say.

"You're a very good mom and wife and daughter," she says, not hearing me. "I know being a working mom can be so hard, and work is very stressful listening to crisis all day, and—"

"Mom..." I can't believe she doesn't even hear me.

"Everything is really hard right now," she continues. "But I promise, it's all going to be just fine. I remember when I first had you and your brother—"

"*Mom*!" I try to interrupt her. She really wants to help, but she's just not getting it. And my anger is boiling over again. I sigh loudly.

"I was tired and working, and as you guys got bigger, it got easier. And you're so good at your work, you're a natural! Just remember that when—"

I tune her out. I wonder if all moms can just talk and never realize their kid wants to say something. I know she cares and means well, but I just can't get a word in, and I'm exhausted from repeating myself. Typically, I'd just give up right here and not say anything. But not today. Today, I'm in apparently in crazy mode.

"*Mom*!" I yell at the top of my lungs. I'm stunned at the sound of my own voice and that I'm shouting at her like this. Who have I turned into? This isn't me. The only other time I remember raising my voice at her was when I was pregnant and hormonal.

"I'm so sick of this! You don't listen! It *is* that bad!" A wave of guilt coats my skin and I feel terrible for yelling at her and cutting her off. But my anger is not quite done spilling over. "No one sees me. *Really* sees me, or even listens. I just can't take it anymore. Everything's just too hard!"

She's too quiet now. Maybe the call got dropped.

"Mom?"

"Yes, I'm here," she says. And she really is.

"I'm sorry, but I'm just losing it right now!" She lets me vent. "Remember when Lily was just born and I used to practically live in the nursery room? She was like a week old, and I was standing there, rocking her to sleep. She was so beautiful and such a good baby. But I remember looking around the room, thinking, 'I'm so exhausted and overwhelmed. How am I supposed to do all of this, and be able to pay my bills, do laundry, go grocery shopping, go to work, go running, do normal things?' I was frozen as if I were trapped under an avalanche and couldn't move. And I felt so alone. I had Dylan, but to be honest, I didn't have him. I felt like it was all on me and has been ever since we got married!"

I catch myself in the middle of this unfair explosion I'm unleashing onto my mom. I can hear the words I would tell my patients: slow down and take a couple of deep breaths. So I do that, feeling my stress push out the oxygen as I'm trying to convince my lungs to breathe. My shoulders loosen up and my head clears up a bit.

"You know more than anyone on this planet how much I like peace and calm and quiet. Maybe it's an introvert thing, I don't know. Or maybe I've been like that since I was…six," I say as I feel my stomach turn. I swear I'm going to throw up.

"Sweetheart, I'm so sorry," my mom says softly. "That should have never happened to you. We can talk about it."

"I'm fine. It's in the past. So long ago. Worse things happen to people. I just felt so ugly and disgusting and filled with shame. Like I became shame. Ugh, whatever. I'm over it." Please just let me keep suppressing it. It makes me cringe to even think about it. It's bad enough I have to keep being reminded of it all with my nightmares.

I roll down the windows, and take in a deep breath. "Mom, I'm just too sensitive for all this."

"For all what?"

"Life. This life I've somehow fallen into." I look out the side window of my car. "How do people do it? How do other introverts do it? Everyone told us having a kid was the next thing we had to do, and that we'd be great parents, and the thoughts of having a baby seemed so sweet when I'd watch parents with their little ones, and their giggles and adorable faces and tiny fingers and miniature clothes. I felt like society's marketing was so deceiving. And we actually got the perfect kid. Lily's perfect. But it's too hard.

"Before Dylan and I got married, I remember we were talking to Jake and Jane after their twins were born. When they kept pushing the 'When are you having kids' questions, I told them I didn't know. I really need my sleep and my routines and quiet. I remember saying to them that the second I don't get sleep, I get grumpy and moody, I can't focus or get anything done. That I get anxiety with loud noises, that I didn't have the money to afford all that is necessary that comes with having a child. They said—everyone said, even *you* said this, too, Mom—that it would be fine, and that it's the best thing in the world and that you just get through it. But I can't do it all by myself," I take another deep breath. "Did I lose you?"

"I'm here. I'm listening," she says.

"This is so hard for me to say, and I feel so disgusted with myself for even thinking these things and feeling these things and saying them out loud. I don't regret having Lily even for a second, but in that moment when I was standing there in the nursery with one-week-old Lily, I feel like I wasn't built to be a mom. Really. I'm not strong enough for it. I felt lied to—by everyone. Even by you, Mom. Why weren't you honest with me? Why didn't you tell me that the insomnia would be excruciatingly painful, that the cries would not subside, and that I'd feel like I was losing my mind? Why didn't you tell me that the worst side of me would come out? That I would never feel like myself again? That I would ultimately be alone in all of this? That I would feel like a complete stranger to myself, yelling and screaming like never before in my entire life? Really, Mom, do you ever even remember *me* yelling and screaming my whole life? Even as a kid?"

I don't wait for her answer. We both know it.

I can't help myself from dominating the conversation. I press on. "I was mute! I had no voice. Now I feel like a totally different person. The stress and panic attacks that I had before having a child were so minuscule compared to what I go through as a mom. No one told me that he would go from my husband who was so active and motivated and working and supporting us *before* we got married, but then after we walked down the aisle that I would be end up in a marriage with a totally different man. That I would never get a break - ever! I wish someone told me to only get married and have a child with someone if I was allowed to work part time and to have a nanny and that he must always provide for us financially. In today's society, women are expected to do it all, and men are lost as to what their roles are anymore. Dylan is a perfect example of that. He knew how to court me, he knew how to be an excellent boyfriend. He knows how to love our daughter.

"But with me being so independent and striving for career goals and earning more money throughout the years, working hard and long hours, it seems as though he doesn't know where his place is. But why can't he also work just as hard? Why does he have to take me for granted? How could he sit back and take the money and claim that it's ours, when all he's doing is figuring out how to spend it on alcohol, and he didn't work for it and he isn't sharing half of the responsibilities at a job or at home?

I think I wouldn't have as much resentment if I'd come home after work to a nice meal every night and him already having gone to the market, and done laundry and cleaned the house and picked up Lily from daycare, and helped feed her, bathe her, and put her to bed. But instead I do every single one of those things, and he just sits back and wants *more!*"

I'm exhausted from speaking for longer than ever at one time.

"I had no idea you felt so alone." My mom's voice is soft, and she sounds so sad. "You're always smiling, and telling me how well things are going at home and work. I just never knew. I'm so sorry."

I come back to reality, turn on my car, and the clock flashes, reminding me that I'm inevitably going to be late for work. Of course. I sigh and roll my eyes, which are probably going to get stuck up there if I have one more day like this.

It usually takes me forever to squeeze out of my parking space and escape the ant farm that is my morning school routine. But because of my flip-out this morning, the school traffic has passed and I coast out of the neighborhood. "Mom, I'm super late to work already. I have to go. Can I call you later?"

"Oh, of course. Please tell me if there is anything I can do to—"

I cut her off. "I'm sorry, I really can't do this right now. I love you."

"Oh, ok. I love y—"

I press *End* as fast as my finger can reach the button. I can't afford another minute of this emotional thunderstorm.

Chapter Five:

Stunning

I turn right and land at a dead stop on 10th Street, then we inch our way forward, and finally get onto Wilshire Boulevard, only to make it to another complete standstill. There must be an accident. We're not even moving more than five miles an hour, as we crawl to our respective destinations. I'm glancing at my phone, trying to look at the balance on my bank account to see if I have to make a transfer from my savings so my checking account isn't negative again.

How is this happening? I did everything right. I went to college, got my degree, haven't stopped working since I was 17, got married to a good guy who had a job and a degree. How am I stressing right now about needing to transfer $50 so that I don't get hit with another overdraft fee?

I glance up and my bumper smashes into the car ahead of me with a loud thunk. *You're kidding me!* As my vision adjusts, I see my car kissing the back of a brand new Maserati. Great.

The next thing I know, I hear the most alluring voice, and my whole body feels tingly. We'll call her Stunning for now, since it's the only suitable name. Stunning is the owner of the Maserati that just formally introduced itself to the tip of my car.

Did someone press slow motion on this scene, mute all the other cars' engines and that guy honking behind me? I can smell her Jo Malone perfume from all the way over here, inside my off-white ride. My subconscious chose this shade of paint over the years by insisting a car wash remain one of the neglected items on my to-do list that gets rolled over to the next day and the next, and never gets crossed off.

My eyes stay hooked onto Stunning's lips. Is she really a foot away from my face? She invites me in with her wavy mocha-colored hair down to her waist, light brown eyes and glowing smile. I feel pulled towards her and transported into a tingly daydream. Butterflies flitter in my stomach and I'm intoxicated by her scent.

The driver behind me lays on the horn. *Thank you, Sir.* My slow motion love scene is officially over.

She tilts her head a little, and looks at her bumper and then at mine, while I'm frozen there like an idiot.

"You know what? It's not a big deal. Can you promise me something?"

She takes the wind out of me. *My God, anything you want.* "Um yes?" I whisper.

"That neither of us will look at our phones while we're driving, ok?" she says.

I'm embarrassed. Texting and driving is just as bad as drunk driving, isn't it? My shame won't let me make eye contact.

I step out of the car and get a better look at her bumper for the first time, and I gasp. My face is doing that twisted thing I hate that it does anytime I'm caught not being perfect. My cheeks are flushed with a perfect shade of bright red. I still can't even look at her, the highest level my eyes will reach is that mashed-up black bumper.

"Hey," her voice is like a cool mint I put in my mouth and I can feel her in my lungs. "It's gonna be ok." Her smile is gentle and softens me. My eyes meet hers.

"Really," I breathe out. I tuck my hair behind my ear nervously. "I should give you something. You know, just in case."

A car flies by, laying down on the horn. I jump a bit as he startles me out of my trance.

I proceed to tack on another layer of embarrassment, because this encounter's not quite awkward enough yet. I get back into my car and lean over to the glove compartment. My hand reaches in and grabs a stack of business cards—not my registration, not my driver's license, no, that would be too logical and appropriate. I hand all twenty or so cards to her.

Stunning looks down at my cards in her hand. "It's nice to meet you, Jelina. I'm... intrigued." Her eyes are serious, as if she's studying me like an art piece at The Getty.

"Ok, um. Thank you?" That's all my brain is allowing me to articulate right now.

She smiles, nods and gets into her car and disappears back to her life - and out of what feels like a dream. My skin feels her aura, as if she just took an ice cube and ran it slowly along my arms, across the back of my neck and down my spine.

Chapter Six:

Panic

Tick...tick...tick...tick.

It's a momentary pause in our session. I know Kim all too well by now. She's gathering her thoughts, taking comfort in the slow ticks of the clock, and savoring the silence—something quite rare in her life outside of these four walls. Kim has been sitting on that couch at one p.m. every Thursday for a little over two years. She's one of my most punctual patients. In fact, I get a little worried if the clock reads 12:58 p.m. and my call light isn't on yet.

I glance over her shoulder. We have 27 more minutes left in our session. A fire truck next door wails its siren, announcing to all of us on Ocean Avenue and Cali Street that it's leaving the station on a mission. Neither Kim nor I flinch. It's a sad truth, but we hear these sirens at least every other session, so we don't skip a beat.

Her gaze is on her shoes, as her feet rest on the flowery footstool.

"Do you ever wonder if you're living the wrong life?" ... *and I guess she's ready to begin.*

"Can you say more?" I hand her back the question.

"Like, I think about my life. I sit indoors all day. My boss doesn't care about who I am. I'm replaceable. What am I even doing?"

"What would you prefer your life to look like?" I ask.

"I thought by now I'd at least be married with a kid and have a house. You know, something fulfilling," she says.

"What leads you to believe those things will fulfill you?"

"Common sense."

"Ouch. Alright, I hear you," I say. Her passive aggressiveness leaves me with a little sting of shame. I channel Professor Burgeon from college. He used to tell us to pay attention to what we feel in the room. It might be what the client's feeling. "I'm curious about something."

Kim's arms are a bit tense as she hugs her pillow against her stomach. She's listening - I think.

"I'm curious if underneath all of this… if you're questioning your worth and value as you compare yourself to your friends as you go to their weddings or baby showers or hear them talk about the houses they're looking at?"

"Yeah, I have to say, it sucks being a bridesmaid. It's getting old."

From my periphery I notice my phone is blowing up with notifications. They're from a random number, and they're not stopping. But, of course, I know whom they're from. He's sending Bible verses and pictures of us together when I was a kid. The notifications won't stop scrolling across my phone. I'm trying hard to stay focused on Kim but my eyes are pulled towards these images. I feel a bullet of shame shoot through me.

"I feel shame and worthless," I hear her say, but it's if she's so far away.

I force my vision to find Kim in this office again. I see her face now, but my ears haven't caught up. I can only catch bits of what she's saying about her inner critic and negative self talk. The rest is muffled like I'm wearing noise-cancelling headphones. I see her mouth moving, and I'm trying to concentrate and make out what she's saying, but I am frozen by this wave of dizziness that's come over me.

I interrupt her mid-sentence. "Kim, can you hold on a second? I'm feeling a little dizzy. I just need a moment." There are two of her—maybe even a third now, and my silencing headphones are less snug.

"Sure?" She's thrown off too. Her silhouette is visible from my periphery, and I've disrupted her flow. She's leaning forward now on the edge of the couch, oozing concern. "Jelina, are you okay?"

"Strange. I don't know why I'm feeling dizzy all of a sudden." I feel guilty that I've switched into the one in the vulnerable chair. I make a failed attempt at standing up to refill my mug. My legs buckle as soon as I'm on my feet, so I drop back into my chair. I can hardly keep my eyes on Kim, but I manage to push out the words, "I need some air," as I'm hyperventilating. She opens the sliding glass door, leaves the office for a minute, and comes back with a cup of water. I can feel myself trying to keep my eyes from seeing double. Then it hits me. I know exactly what this is. It's taken a much different shape this afternoon with the dizziness, *and* in front of a patient. Those are firsts. A panic attack and vertigo at the same time, this is nuts. The room won't stop spinning. Damn it! I can't believe this is happening right now, in the middle of a session!

As my panic attack grabs the reins, and my vicious vertigo subsides, I feel the all-too-familiar powerlessness, as if I'm six years old again. I can't stop hyperventilating. My heart feels like it's going to jump out of my chest. My hands are shaking. My body feels like I'm in ice cold water.

It's just a panic attack, ride it out, I think to myself, trying to use a strategy I teach my patients. Between breaths, I slide into surrender. *Just let go.* I close my eyes and breathe for a moment, giving myself permission to sink into my chair, and just be human.

A stream of images flashes across my mind, as if I'm on a train watching the scenery go by. My breath is the rapid chugging of the engine on the tracks.

Chug chug-chug chug-chug. My breath follows the pace and rhythm.

I rub the healing cut on my hand. Still shots of me pass like mental scenery on this express train: me yelling at Dylan, losing it in the car, another one of me looking through the peephole seeing the gun pointed at me and the camera clicking pictures, an exhausted me soothing a crying infant Lily, the sweet little blonde girl sitting on the kitchen floor.

Chug chug-chug chug-chug.

My breath follows the pace of my mental train. The scenery keeps going by in my mind, slower now. The little blonde girl is writing in her notebook.

Chug…chug-chug…

The mental train has slowed to almost a stop. As my panic attack slows down and my daydream continues, I see the pages in the little girl's book: a drawing with sparkles of light reflecting on the sea water. She turns the glittery page and shows me another drawing of an island in the sea.

My eyes open, and my mind is back in the office with Kim. "What the hell, Jelina?" she asks, wide-eyed.

"Seriously," I agree with her. I look over at the clock.

2:02. "Let's pick back up again next week."

Chapter Seven:

Her

That was by far the most bizarre thing that's ever happened to me in a session in all these years. Wow. I open my work bag and check my phone.

Dylan: You meeting the girls today?

I type back.

Me: In a bit. Sunkissed Cafe. Hey, I got in a little fender bender this morning.

Dylan: Dammit!

Me: It's fine. No big deal

Dylan: We can't afford this right now

Me: I'm ok, the car's ok. The other car was worse, but she said not to worry about it

Dylan: Cool. Can you stop by the cleaners and pick up my dry cleaning after work

Me: You can't do it?

Dylan: I have a project to work on all night

Me: Fine, I can get it tomorrow

Dylan: Thanks. How was Lily this morning

Me: Sweet, quiet. She loves Miss Kayla

Dylan: Good. I miss her already. My little Lilykin

Me: She's adorable. It would be nice if you dropped her off some mornings

Dylan: Babe, you know I'm not a morning person. I'm our night shift, remember?

I roll my eyes.

Me: I have to go. Meeting the girls.

Dylan: K, love you babe

I set my phone down and pull the spiral note-book out of my bag that I'd tossed in it earlier.

I flip it open to where I left off...

September 20, 2016

    We closed escrow today. Finally. Damn that entire process was so stressful, it's almost hard to take in the excitement. But our house is perfect, especially since we've been talking about having a baby. And we're going to start rotating our weekly wine and cheese dinners with Jake and Jane, and of course, Helen and Sarah, too.

I skip chunks of pages...

July 12, 2019

    I told him I'm tired of our money stress and that all the pressure is on me to cover the bills now because he keeps quitting jobs and changing careers. I was hopeful when we met and he was studying law and I thought it was the right thing to do to be supportive when he ended up changing his major and decided he didn't want to be a lawyer anymore, and got his liberal arts degree. I liked that he was into wanting to teach for a while, and to follow his passions and live a more inspired and free life, and I got a bit anxious when he opened his own surf shop and became a surf instructor. He loved it though, and was the most charming, coolest surfer in town. But after he got tired of the cattiness on the waves, he sold the business and insisted on getting his personal training certification. When that lost its spark, he quit. We've poured most of our savings (that is, my savings from before I met him) into each of these ventures, not to mention all the student loans we racked up. We keep fighting so much lately about how I didn't want the pressure of carrying all the financial burden, and I need him to contribute something to my income, which he calls "our" income, when all he's doing is spending what I'm making! This was a discussion that I never remember having when we talked about our lives together. I'm such a minimalist and he's so materialistic. I wish I'd gotten the memo to never share bank accounts. He has no tolerance for discomfort whatsoever, and demands to have everything handed to him straight from the top. So instead of applying for any paying job, he pushed and pushed for us to take out another loan so that he could switch careers yet again, going back to law school to get his JD. All these years later, and he still hasn't finished. He just has no patience and doesn't like people telling him what to do. I know this has everything to do with how he was raised, but it still doesn't make marriage easy, when I'm the one who has to hold down the fort. He spends all day hanging out with other people under the guise of studying and "doing projects" and they are so loud when they come over, leaving their beer cans and crumbs everywhere. I try to force myself not to clean up after them, but I left it all there and after a four days, he told me, "Don't worry about it, I'll do it." It never happened. If I don't do it, no one will. And I can't live in a pig sty.

July 13, 2019

We just had one of our biggest fights. He's been insisting on getting a drone so he could sit back and take videos around our house!! I'm not even making this up. I feel like his mom, not his wife. I can't believe this is even a conversation. I'm so livid right now and I feel so alone in this marriage!!

Uggg. My stomach is turning. I flip past more pages...

August 2, 2019

Right when I walked into work, Mel asked me again if everything's ok. I hate when she does that. She always asks me right before I have to run my grief group. And then I cry for no reason every time, and have panic attacks and it's impossible to pull it together before I have to lead the group. I never even have

the strength or time to talk to her. And I'm so embar-
rassed. How on earth can I even admit that my own
marriage is a mess? I feel awful, but I ended up mus-
tering up the courage somehow to tell her to stop ask-
ing if I'm ok, because it's too hard to gather my com-
posure every time right before patients walk in and I
have to run group. I don't even know who I am any-
more. I don't wear makeup like I used to, the clothes I
want, or do my hair how I prefer. I've lost myself.
Lately, Dylan has a negative comment about every
little thing, and he's not even taking care of himself
anymore, but he finds time to criticize me. His drink-
ing is getting concerning and every time I bring it up
he gets defensive. He's so critical and controlling! I
wear the shade of lipstick he insists upon, the style of
haircut, the clothes he prefers. I just scream!! Why
can't I stand up for myself? What happened to you
treating me like the queen like you did before we got
married!?

Tears are falling onto my cheeks. I miss how
we were at the beginning. I keep flipping pages.

September 18, 2020

    I went to my session with Lauren yesterday. She diagnosed me with Generalized Anxiety Disorder and said I'm a codependent love addict and an enabler. Great. My own therapist knows I'm a mess. For so long I was the classic case of being caught in the high of the fantasy cycle with him from early on. Which means at some point, like with any addiction, I was bound to come down from the high, face reality, and go through withdrawal. Maybe that's what this is now. I'm detoxing from my fantasy. The euphoric recall is over. I told Lauren how I keep getting panic attacks. It's all the running around I am doing: working straight through my lunches, cooking, cleaning, taking care of Lily on my own from the moment I wake up until before I go to bed, because Dylan doesn't want to wake up early and is always "looking for another job" (aka sleeping or hungover). I can't even take time off or quit like he does every year because he's just bored with a job, because someone needs to make money to pay our bills. No one's asking me to change her or bathe her or feed her. Can't he see that I'm the one paying our bills and taking care of our child and cooking our meals while he sleeps all day and drinks all night, and I clean up after him? He had the nerve to tell me that I've been slacking on cleaning the house last weekend, and not doing it like I used to. Serious-ly?! I need us to be a team. He completely changed after we walked down that aisle. His drive, motivation, being a true partner—all gone. He's cheated me. Now I feel like we've become strangers. No, worse than that — the worst versions of ourselves.

Lauren suggested I start asking Dylan for help. Why I didn't apply that common sense years ago is beyond me. My guess is I was busy trying to be the perfect wife and not let him be uncomfortable. But last night, I decided to take her advice and stop assuming he would just have empathy or be a considerate person. I removed my superwoman cape and asked him to alternate nights we bathed Lily.

At first, it was sweet hearing the bath water splashing and the giggles between them. I was finally resting on that sofa for the very first time; not working, cleaning, cooking, not doing a single thing. It was heavenly. I closed my eyes, let my body sink into the sofa, and felt such a difference sitting still...even my mind could rest for a bit. I was completely relaxed and motionless.

But as I sat in the quiet living room finally doing absolutely nothing for the first time, it all hit me. The anger rushed through my body. While I was run-ning around like a chicken with its head cut off, he lives in this luxury of what I so desperately long for: utter relaxation.

God! I've never felt more rage. This is what he does, all day, every day on that very sofa while I'm running servicing his every need in this one-sided re-lationship, stressed out of my mind, working to pay our bills, go grocery shopping, cook, clean, then do Lily's bath time and bedtime and he does this: sit and relax all day in his pajamas, complain that I'm not cleaning the house as well as I did in the past."

Rage, utter rage. I didn't sign up for this. I didn't ask to be the breadwinner or his servant.

My resentment is doing push-ups, growing stronger with each passing day. His drinking has gone from socially on weekends to a couple glasses of Whiskey most nights. He's draining our bank accounts with his addictions and gluttony. Of course I can't say these things. I'd die if I made him feel badly, and I don't want to fight. He's my husband, I have to sup-port him, and I know he's trying.

I skip more pages.

...I know in my gut that Lily is as shy as she is because she feels our tension. She's still not toilet-trained. Her Christmas program was last night and

she stood off to the side completely still. All the other kids were smiling, singing and dancing, and there was our sweet little Lily, not uttering a word or moving an inch, just frozen in her familiar stance: head down, furrowed brows, chewing on her finger, silent. I couldn't stand seeing her so uncomfortable, so I went up and took her off stage and had her sit on my lap.

I flip some more.

...I wish I can say to him "If you don't change, I'm leaving." But I can't even imagine that. I can't break up Lily's home.

I turn to the last entry, one I wrote a couple months ago.

April 7, 2023

I'm livid!! I saw 9 patients back to back today and worked through lunch typing up notes. When I finally got home tonight, I had Lily in one hand and a bag of groceries in the other. He didn't move his eyes from the laptop, was still in his pajamas from the night before and asks me, "Did you deposit your patients' checks from today?" You're a lazy, selfish mooch! I raged at him in my mind. I wish I could say this to him, but I just can't.

Ugg. I have to get out of here. I close my notebook, grab my keys and wristlet.

*   *   *   *

Sunkissed Café is packed, but Sarah and Helen make me feel like we're the only ones in this place. The Italian music they have playing is soothing my unsettled heart.

I stir my tea a bit, still frustrated.

"Babe, are you trying to break the cup?" Sarah teases me. "Don't get me wrong, it's better watching you be angry than sad all the time."

"You guys, I'm telling you, the most excitement I have in my life is when I'm daydreaming. Remember, when I used to have those wild fantasies?"

"I'm all ears," Helen winks at me.

My anger is slipping away as I visit my mental getaway.

"How can I forget?" Helen gets a pen out and hands it to me with a napkin. "You'd talk about that retreat so much I still remember the little maps you'd draw on napkins."

I take the pen and let my mind float into dreamland for a bit.

"There'd be huge open air tents with signs, and little pathways to each of them. A Raw Room, a Focus Room, a Nourish Room. And I'd put a fire pit right here in the middle."

I point my pen to the scribble of flames in the center of the napkin.

"And people could play guitar, and paint, and have a safe healthy fun place to go any time. It would have all the perks of an addiction treatment center, but available to anyone. I'd have paddle-boards hanging on racks and groups could paddle out and do meditation on the water. But now, my dreams are more freaking me out than anything."

"What do you mean?" Sarah asks.

"The other night, I had this vivid dream—a nightmare, I guess. My stalker was on the other side of my front door at home, just standing there pointing a gun in my direction and holding his phone up, taking pictures nonstop. And I had a knife in my hand."

Helen puts her hand on my arm. "J, I'm sorry these nightmares are coming back again."

"It's pretty bizarre. But the even crazier thing was just now, in session. My patient was talking, and I started to see out of the corner of my eye all these notifications, texts, and photos of me just coming in non-stop on my phone. It was like they came from my dream, my stalker behind the front door with a gun pointed at me and taking photos, and all the photos were coming into my phone right there in the middle of a session! And I had a freaking panic attack and vertigo right there in front of my patient."

"That's a trip," Helen says.

"The panic attacks aren't the worst of it. You guys are going to think I'm crazy, but I think my anxiety is making me hallucinate. I keep freaking out seeing pictures of me when I was in high school. It was the worst time of my life. This is really embarrassing to even say out loud but remember how shy and insecure I was back then? I had such low self-esteem, I cut out all my pictures and basically hid from the world those entire four years."

"I think you should think about taking meds," Sarah says. "They've done wonders for me."

Helen replies, "No, what she needs is some seriously hot night."

"How's that department going?" Sarah asks, spreading fig on a slice of Brie with a knife.

I would usually do the same, savoring the sweet and salty taste, but I have no appetite.

"Eh. I don't even think about that right now. I just need Dylan to quit making excuses, stop drinking and keep a job so I can stop burning out."

"I thought you guys tried couples therapy?" Sarah asks.

I roll my eyes. "We tried it once about a few months ago. He didn't want to go and said it would be a waste of time, but I told him we're fighting too much and Lily's definitely feeling our tension and that I just can't keep living like this. So we went."

"Is Lily still having accidents?" Helen asks.

I nod. "Only on the weekends, never at school. And my therapist says her shyness and separation anxiety is clearly because Dylan and I aren't ok."

"How did the session go when he went with you?" asks Sarah.

"Pointless. Dylan was annoyed being there and acted like he knew more than my therapist. She asked both of us to say what we each take responsibility for regarding the problems in our marriage. We were both so frustrated, and so busy blaming each other, that she just jumped in and told me that I play the martyr, I'm a people pleaser, and I'm codependent. She said I'm playing the victim and need to take responsibility and have my voice. She told Dylan he acts entitled, is boundary-less, and creates chaos with his addictions, which pushes me away. She said neither of us communicates clearly to the other person, and that he responds to stress by 'acting out' and indulging himself, while I respond by 'acting in' and neglecting myself."

Helen adds, "That's depressing. How about a threesome? Maybe adding some spice will make you both chill out."

"Thanks, that'll make things a lot less complicated." I'm rarely sarcastic, but I can't help myself.

"Well, all kidding aside, something has to change," Sarah says. "We love you, J. And you're just not ok. You're too skinny, you never eat, you always look exhausted, you work harder than anyone I know. And look, your panic attacks are getting *worse*, and you're stressed about money all the time. I'm afraid you're going to end up in the hospital with a nervous breakdown, or in the grave."

"What am I supposed to do? He's a good guy, we're not abusing each other. Fine, he drinks too much and isn't working. But so many people have it worse. I have no choice. I can't quit my job, we have Lily. This is the life I signed up for, and I just have to deal with it," I say. They just don't get it.

"This isn't the 1950s. You're never stuck. You always have a choice. Sometimes it doesn't feel like it, but you do," Sarah snaps back.

I let that sink in for a moment. The very thought of the word divorce in my mind makes me cringe and feel like a complete failure. And there isn't a concrete reason to actually leave. He isn't having an affair, he doesn't abuse me. And there are just so many unknowns, starting with how it would affect Lily. I think about her, then I remember the little girl in my dream.

"Oh! I remember this other part of my dream!" I'm desperate to change this depressing sub-ject. "I can't believe I didn't mention this. There was this little girl sitting on the kitchen floor. She wasn't Lily, though. She had glasses. She was writing some-thing in a notebook. Anyway, I keep thinking about her. I think she was at one of the lectures I did at the elementary school last winter."

I put my cup of tea down, lean back in my chair, and tie my hair in a low bun. While I'm adding one last bobby pin to secure it, Helen touches the bruises on the backs of my arms with one finger. "What's this?"

The blood rushes to my face. My arms drop down and without the last bobby pin in place, my hair loosens a bit. "It's nothing. Dylan was driving me crazy again, and I just lost my mind."

Sarah's voice rises; she doesn't care if there's an audience.

"*What the hell, J?* He did this to you?!"

I'm mortified. I want to disappear. "What? No! Dylan would never put a hand on me. Ever. I'm so embarrassed. This was me. I can't hit anyone else or anything else. He just pissed me off again, coming home drunk, and I have to do everything. Everything! I work my ass off all day, cook for him, clean, do his laundry, take care of Lily. And I can't yell at him in front of Lily, and he was passed out this morning after almost puking on me. Anyway, I dropped her off at school and the second I got back in the car I just lost it and yelled and cried and finally got all my anger out."

They both stare at me with shock and sympathy in their eyes. I loathe this feeling. My polished wall is crumbling right before my very eyes. Vulnerability stings like hell.

"We're so worried about you, babe. This can't keep going like this," Helen says to me.

Out of nowhere, a strong ocean breeze glides through the room. Everything is moving in slow motion and I'm completely rescued from the intense moment I was just having. My whole body and mind shift into an entirely different gear.   Somehow the temperature rises about ten degrees. I'm in a whole other dimension right now, and Helen and Sarah seem to be carrying on their conversation very far away from me. I feel a rush throughout my body, as if someone grazed their hand across my skin, from the top of my face down my entire body, and I'm tingly all over.

Stunning.

I hear her voice on the other side of the restaurant. I think I smell her perfume, but that can't be right. My heart's beating faster, and my palms are sweating.

The whole place seems to go quiet, and there she is. I thought I'd never see her again. She's standing in a spotlight in the middle of the restaurant. Every syllable that passes her lips sends a vibration straight down my spine. Her eyes meet mine, and I can't unlock my gaze.

Helen waves her hand in front of my face. "Babe, hello? Where are you right now?"

The room returns to its previous volume, and I see Stunning talking to the entire restaurant staff near the kitchen. Is she the new owner?   My hands are shaking, but I'm not nervous. Or maybe I am. I don't know. I feel high right now. Maybe Sarah slipped some edibles onto the cheese platter without me know-ing. My phone chimes—it's 3:50 p.m. I inhale deeply.

"I love you guys, but I have to run." I look in my wristlet for a twenty, but all I have is a five-dollar bill.

"This one's on me, ladies," Sarah says.

"I'll pay you back," I reply.

The waitress returns, peeking at the check holder before closing it and placing it on the table right in front of me. She sets it down on top of a to-go box. With a smirk, she says, "Have a nice afternoon, Jelina."

"Jelina?" Sarah glances at her, leans across the table and grabs the check holder. She looks it over for a few seconds, sits back and smiles. Her elbows rest on the arms of the chair, fingertips holding up what looks like my own blue business card with handwrit-ing scribbled on it.

"Well, none of us have to pay a thing, and someone's got an admirer."

Sarah hands me my own business card. On the back is handwritten: *Jelina, you intrigue me. 8 p.m. tonight: 27 La Brea Ave. Text me when you get there 555-2010. —Natalia xo*

My heart's racing so fast and I'm warm, and like I'm floating a bit. I feel drunk or high, but so much better.

Natalia.

Even her name is pretty.

Helen leans over and takes a look at the card. "Who's this? I like her already."

"It's a long story," I say. How we met isn't, but what she makes me feel is. I look around and don't see her anywhere around the restaurant. I feel stalked, but this time I like it.

Chapter Eight:

Don't Neglect Happiness

I walk along Ocean Avenue, holding my card between my fingertips. *Natalia.* She had this between her fingertips just moments ago. I bring it up to my nose and breathe it in, closing my eyes for a second and I smile.

I hear the guitar guy strumming along, and put my card in my purse. I set the to-go box I brought from the café beside him, and walk up the stairs to my office with a few minutes to spare.

My call light is on, but I'll give myself permission to take a mini mental vacation. I have enough time for a short meditation. I take out my phone, lie down on the shag rug, and set the timer for two minutes. I enter my mental Focus Room, hit *Start* and close my eyes, letting my lips part and rest slightly open. I orient myself to the very present moment, on this very day, in this very room. I can feel my lungs expanding and contracting with every breath, my body being held by the ground and the breeze through the open glass door. I let my mind go where it wants, and each time, pull my attention back to my breath. This mini meditation is my oxygen mask lately.

The alarm chimes, and I open my eyes and press *Stop*. My arms stretch over my head, laying flat against the ground. I roll onto my stomach and press up into my mini version of a Vinyasa flow, ending with an inversion—a new pose I'm proud of. As the blood rushes to my head, I return to my feet, and see it's four p.m., right on the dot. For the next two hours, I step into my patients' worlds.

*   *   *   *

My last patient leaves, and I close the door behind him. As I type up my note I get a notification on my phone that he's sent me his payment. I grab my keys and purse and switch off the office light. I stop in my tracks when I remember my card. My heart flutters and I have butterflies in my stomach. I see Natalia's handwriting. I drop my bag to the floor, grab the card, and sit back in my chair. The only light that's coming in is the sunset that's peeking through the blinds of the windows, and a glow from the balcony, with its scenic view of the beach that I never look at when I'm in this office.

I haven't studied my business card for this long, not even when I was sent the proofs to comb through for errors before they printed the final version. But here I sit, under the moonlight. Her hands have held this same card. She actually recognized me today. I can't believe I saw her again. Why does she want to see me? Maybe she wants to file a claim against my insurance for hitting her car. I rub my thumb over her writing.

…you intrigue me…

Is Sarah right? Could this goddess really be hitting on me? That makes no sense. I'm *so* unattractive right now with my permanent stress-face, acne, and tired look. She must see the big rock on my finger.

What's at 27 La Brea? Oh my God! What if it's a romantic room at Malibu Beach Inn? I Google it. It's a grocery store. Maybe she inverted the numbers? She could be dyslexic, you never know. A pawn shop shows up on the searches. That would make her creepy, not mysterious. This woman has shaken up my entire world. What am I doing? I'm really considering meeting her? I don't even know her. I'm *married*. Is this cheating? I need to grab something to make for dinner, and cook, and bath-time and story-time and paperwork...

I text Dylan.

Me: Babe, I'm sorry, but I have a patient crisis and need to go to Cedars Sinai. I don't know when I'll be home. Can you get Lily from daycare? There are leftovers you can warm up. Lily needs to be in bed by 8, ok? Love you

Dylan: That's fine. Love you

I'm officially a horrible person. My husband is home with our kid while I'm over here lying to him doing God knows what.

I inhale deeply. My body is warm again and my heart's beating faster. I turn on the light in my office, and start typing in the numbers from the card and save her name in my phone. Why am I even doing this? Ugh. She said to text her when I get there, but why would she want to meet at the grocery store at eight o'clock at night in the middle of Hollywood?

Does she really think I'm going to drive by myself to meet some random stranger in Hollywood? This is straight out of an '80s horror film. Meanwhile, my fingers have taken the lead, and I have an open text message with the flashing cursor waiting for my next move. My body is damp with nervousness. *Just thank her and cancel graciously.*

Me: Hi Natalia, I got your message. Thank you for the offer, but I can't —

Delete, delete, delete. I can't what? Have dinner at the grocery store, be a willing victim to you kidnapping and murdering me, go with you to a remote island and let you make love to me for hours? I try again.

Me: Hi Natalia, it's Jelina. Wa

Damn it! I hit send by accident. Wa is nothing, a total typo. Want to cancel...Was fantasizing about you...Want to disappear from sheer humiliation

I see the three dots. She's rescuing me from this mental spiral.

Natalia: Jelina, what a pleasant surprise to see you in my restaurant today. Did you like the new cheese platter we added to the menu?

Wow, she's good. The muscles in my legs and arms release the tension they've been holding this entire time.

Me: It was delicious!

I'm lying, as I only nibbled on a few grapes.

She wastes no time and gets straight to her agenda.

Natalia: So, for tonight, keep an open mind and don't be late. The doors to the place I'm taking you to close exactly at 8 o'clock and won't reopen

Wait, she's just assuming that I'm agreeing to this?

Me: Are we going to a show?

Natalia: I can't tell you. It would ruin the thrill of it all. Just don't Google it and don't be late

Because you don't want me to see that we're meeting at the grocery store?

Me: I'm still in my work clothes and I already ate

Another lie; I'm starving!

Me: By the way, I just have to ask. Is this a date? Because I'm sorry, but I really can't. I'm married

I continue to ramble.

Me: I have a husband and kid at home. I'm not that kind of person. I don't meet up with people who look like you in the middle of the night. I don't do anything in the middle of the night for that matter

I—

She interrupts my wave of texts with an actual phone call.

Why are you calling me? Oh my God, I can't talk to you. I hate this. I press Answer. Ugg.

"Hi there." Oh, God. That voice. It sends a tingling rush into my ear. I can almost feel her lips against my neck. I melt. Her voice has now replaced the blood in my veins and is warm and all-consuming.

"Hi," I manage to reply. Beyond that, I'm speechless. She's silenced me with her magic.

Natalia pulls me back in with a calm, "Jelina."

I hold my breath. "Yes?"

"Don't neglect your happiness for anyone. You could live happier beyond your wildest dreams."

I exhale, and her words marinate in my head.

That's my life. My days, my nights. I've lost myself. I'm literally disappearing. I'm ten pounds underweight, burnt out from life, alone in my marriage, feeling like a single mom, angrier, sadder and more exhausted than I've ever been in my life.

"What did you just say?" I just want to hear these words again.

"You deserve to be happy," she says.

Natalia has awoken me from the terrible nightmare I've been living.

Imagine yourself laying down on a bed of flowers in a garden on a warm summer day, bathing in the warm sunlight, and a magical goddess is seductively leaning over you. Do you feel that rush in your chest? Now picture her holding a soaking wet sponge and ever so slowly letting cool water drip and cover you, one inch at a time. Do you feel the tingle in your palms? That's the power of Natalia.

"I'll see you at eight." The words are delivered effortlessly from my desires to hers.

Chapter Nine:

Sound Bath

I press *End* on the phone and it almost slips out of my sweaty hands.

Is this really happening? What's "this" anyway? We're just two people hanging out and getting to know each other. But if it's that innocent, then why does my heart jump every time I think of her, and why does she make me feel like I'm ten years younger and that I can run a 5k right now? I've never felt this pull towards someone, this euphoric rush and tingle throughout my body, this alive—since pre-married Dylan. I unzip my wallet, pull out my eye liner and lip gloss. I freshen up in the mirror behind my office door. As I'm applying lip gloss, I'm trying to figure out for whom I am freshening up. Is it for her? Am I trying to impress her? Or is it for me, because it feels incredible to be desired again? My eyes freeze on my glossy pink lips, and I can feel my panties getting wet without touching them at just the remote possibility that her lips would press against mine. I sigh as I remember the first moment I was pulled into her like this, sitting in my car, mesmerized by her mouth, her voice, her glow, her scent.

I shake out of the spell, close up the office and get to my car. I'm pretty early, but we all know that in L.A. that doesn't mean you'll make it to your destination on time. It's standard to add 20 minutes extra for traffic, finding parking, studying the signs so you don't get a ticket, and finally walking to wherever you're going from wherever you parked, or I can just valet I guess. She said I couldn't be late. I'm so flattered that she's even put this much effort into planning tonight's date—or whatever this is. The last time I felt this way was when Dylan and I were dating. Everything we do now, I'm always the one to plan it all, every step of the way—the time, what we're doing, offering options because nobody wants to initiate, but somehow they're also very picky.

Tonight is already light-years different than anyone I've "met up" with. She's already done all the thinking and planning for us. God knows what she has in store for tonight, and hopefully I come out of it in one piece. I honestly don't know what's come over me to even be in this car right here, right now, on a Thursday night, driving to meet a stunning woman I met in a car accident. This couldn't get any further from my predictable life.

I follow my navigation app's voice. I make a left turn and she informs me, "In point five miles, your destination will be on your right." I arrive at the corner of La Brea and Third. "You have reached your destination." Yup, I look around. Google was right. There's the grocery store. Shockingly, I find a parking spot within a couple of minutes. She has magic powers indeed

I check my face in the rear view mirror one more time. I actually don't look tired. I smile as I realize I'm moments away from being alone with her for the first time, and I step out of the car. She's nearby, I can just feel it. I text her.

Me: I'm here

Natalia: I see you :) I have a little surprise. Close your eyes

I smile as I take the risk of closing my eyes in the middle of a parking lot in Hollywood at night. Is this even real right now? What am I doing? The swirl of excitement and fear is exhilarating. I wait about ten seconds, and I can hear her steps approaching from behind. Am I the biggest idiot on the planet? Why didn't I text Helen or Sarah where I was going in case I end up dead in a ditch somewhere? This murder news story will go viral tomorrow. Or worse, I wonder how long it would even take for anyone to notice I was dead.

I feel Natalia's arms wrap around me from behind. Her breasts press against my back. Her lips are beside my ear and she whispers, "You made it."

I breathe in the smell of her skin as her arm lays across my collarbone, and my skin tingles at the sound of her whispers in my ear. Without my permission, my hand reaches up and touches her arm. Her skin is as smooth as silk.I say nothing, of course, because how could anyone even know how to respond to all that?

She releases me, and I turn around to face her, tilting my head up as her eyes meet mine. She hands me a hot tea and small sandwich. How does she know what I like?

"I know you had a long day and I thought you might be hungry," she says.

"Hi." I feel my cheeks flush. "Thank you for these, and for tonight," I say. *For tonight, really J?* I can't believe how weird I get around her. I give lectures to rooms of 200 people like I'm talking to my best friend, but put me in front of this woman, and I turn into an awkward teenager. I take the tea in one hand and the sandwich in the other, lean in to give her a hug, and spill tea on her top. "Wow, I am so sorry!" I'm stuck with my hands full and I'm looking around for something to wipe it with. I'm sure I look like I'm fumbling a football right now.

Natalia doesn't even flinch, casually takes the tea back from me, and sets it down on the trunk of the car next to us. She's holding me right now, both of her arms gently wrapped around my body, and she's calming me with her gaze. Her light brown eyes soothe me instantly, and my own thoughts get muted along with my swirling feelings and all the city's sounds. My attention gets sucked into her, and we drop down into our quiet cozy cave, alone together. She says, "Tonight's all about you, Jelina. Just relax and enjoy the ride."

My head's tilted back as I look up at her. I'm fighting back tears. This is the first time in a really long time that I can remember feeling taken care of, that I can sit back and be held and pampered. That's always my job with everyone in my life. Her lips are just a few inches from mine. My eyes beg her: *please kiss me, please kiss me...*

She replies with a smile. "Let's start walking. We can't be late." She grabs the tea and takes my hand.

We walk hand in hand, taking turns sharing the sandwich, entering random shops as she teases me about where we're going. I think it's adorable that she's stalling by having us enter and exit clothing stores, boutiques, and speciality shops, playing with me like this was her night's plan. After hundreds of steps, we enter the Zen Meditation Center.

There's a long line of people, and we inch our way forward, sharing our tea, which is cold by now, but neither of us seems to mind. The yogi checking us all in behind the counter is stoic. She seems to be about 20, with tattoos on her arms and bracelets that clank like chimes when she moves. The line's moving pretty fast.

"Name, please?" 20 asks, her eyes glued to the computer screen. Is she annoyed that we're here? I thought meditation centers were of the Make Love Not War vibe.

"Natalia and Jelina," Natalia answers. With just those three words, she manages to melt 20's cold wall. I'm watching it happen right in front of me. Her face softens as she takes in all that is Natalia. Her eyes twinkle, and she's chewing on her pen, flashing her bright smile, and I swear she just giggled.

"Sign in right here, please." 20 is now blushing and stuttering; she's entranced by Natalia. "Have either of you, um, ever been to a sound bath before?" She can't stop herself from lusting after Natalia, and this is ridiculous, but I feel a sting of jealousy in my chest.

Natalia stands close to me, knowing exactly how I'm feeling and what to do about it. My heart is pounding as I realize her forearm is pressing against mine and she's leaning into me, her mouth near my neck. I'm frozen while I'm looking straight ahead, as Natalia whispers into my ear, "Have you?"

I shake my head, and the word *No* somehow escapes my mouth as I exhale deeply. 20 drops her pen to the floor, and doesn't bother picking it back up.

"You're incredible," I say to Natalia, as we're walking away from a spellbound 20. "I've never met anyone like you in my life." What I really want to say is, "I've never wanted anyone so badly in my life."

There are about 15 of us in the lounge area waiting for the sound bath doors to open. Natalia and I relax in plush chairs near the fireplace for a few minutes, drinking mint-flavored water. Conversation is easy with her, and I catch sprinkles of how intelligent and funny she is.

20 steps away from her counter, announcing to the now standing-room-only lounge, "We will begin in about ten minutes. If you need to use the restroom, please do so now. The doors will remain closed and will only re-open when the sound bath is completed in two hours."

I look at Natalia curiously. I'm mesmerized.

20 continues, "Please set your phones to silent mode and remove your shoes before entering, placing them in the wooden cubes against the wall. Namaste." It looks like she's speaking only to Natalia, despite this room packed with meditators. 20 flirts with her eyes and swings her hips as she pulls open the tall wooden doors that encase the sound bath room. *Can you be any more obvious?* I roll my eyes at 20.

"What did you bring me to? Are we taking off our clothes and listening to music underwater?" I ask as we slip off our shoes. So awkward.

"Something like that," she says and takes my shoes, placing them with hers in the empty wooden cubes near us.

I break away from this fantasy for a few seconds and set my phone to silent, as instructed. I text Dylan.

Me: Taking longer than I thought. Don't wait up. Give kisses to Lily from me

In the crowd, Natalia takes my hand but I pull away. Why does it feel strange to me now? I feel a pit of guilt in my stomach. We just held hands for I don't know how many minutes as we walked over here. Maybe it's because we're standing still, shoulder to shoulder with people all around us. I've never once stepped outside of my marriage. I have never so much as kissed anyone else, or felt anything close to romantic feelings for anyone else, since I met Dylan. I'm devoted to him. I love him. Maybe Natalia is in my life for some purpose, to help wake me up, to help repair my marriage. Is being here even considered cheating? What is cheating, anyway? Texting, holding hands, sharing a sandwich, kissing?

Is it cheating that Dylan barely budges to help me after a long day of work? Is it cheating that he doesn't contribute to household income? Is it cheating that for exactly three times the during our first weeks together he brought me to my knees with blazing orgasms from his passionate mouth, and then just stopped and withdrew that part of himself for the remainder of our seven years together? I don't know the answer, but I do know I can't keep living how I've been living—or rather, dying how I've been dying. And I know this feels good right now, being here in this moment. It feels incredible to be taken care of, to feel passion, desire, respect, and so alive! I want that with Dylan. With that, I give myself permission to let go and feel alive for the first time in years.

I take Natalia's hand, and she strokes her thumb against mine. A surge of electricity runs from my hands straight into my chest and signals my brain to deliver pools of sweat to my palms. My body stiffens with insecurity, and I'm about to apologize when she takes my hand in both of hers, massaging it with her thumbs, and carrying it closer to her face as she sweetly blows her cool breath onto my palms. How does she do this? She takes me from feeling insecure to nurtured instantly. She gets me.

The tall wooden doors creak open. We follow the herd of meditators into the massive room. The lighting is a blend of gold and pink. A sea of black mats are lined up neatly, with brightly colored pillows and blankets sprawled throughout the room. At the front, a woman sits cross-legged and barefoot, wearing a dark blue top, a long white skirt, and several necklaces dangling to her belly. She's holding a large wooden mallet and has a bronze Tibetan singing bowl resting in her lap.

"Welcome everyone. I'm Rosie, and I'll be guiding you today. This is your own unique journey. So find a mat, sit down or lay down, keep your eyes opened or closed, just get cozy. We have a full house tonight."

I look around for the gigantic community bathtub I had envisioned when I was imagining what this whole sound bath thing was about. The only water in the room is a gently trickling backlit waterfall in the far corner. I see various instruments set up around the room: singing bowls, tuning forks, drums, a beautiful harp, wind chimes, and several other things that I've never seen before.

Natalia sweeps her hand through the air, inviting me to choose where I'd like us to be. I find two adjacent mats near the exposed brick wall. We crawl onto our mats, spread a large blanket across both of our legs, and adjust our pillows. Rosie glides her mallet around the outside rim of the singing bowl, and soft tones float throughout the vast space. Her presence commands the room to quiet down. One by one, chatter turns into whispers. I look at Natalia. She's gazing up at the brushed nickel tiles on the ceiling. She feels my eyes on her and glances in my direction. She mouths "Hi" as the room has now fallen silent. I smile and sneak a peek down by our hands. There are precisely 10 inches between our fingertips, and only about four inches between our mats. My heart flutters. I breathe in this moment. I can live in this dream for a while.

I let my eyes close, and my body melts into the mat. This moment feels unreal. I don't have to do a single thing for the next two hours; not work, not cook, not clean, not pay a bill, not listen to Dylan's demands, not one thing. All I have to do is lay here in this tranquil room and let go of all my tension.

Rosie is now blending the music from the wind chimes and tuning forks. I can sense her walking around the room as I hear her getting closer and further from us. My mind is swirling with images. In my mind's eye I see Lily holding onto my leg, and us in bed as I trace her face. I see my dad stalking me in my recurring nightmares and daydreams, feeling him watching me, standing behind me, pointing a gun at me, taunting me with endless pictures. I see Dylan on the sofa in his pajamas, drinking, vomiting, playing with his drone. I see my coworker asking if I'm ok. I see my therapist's worried eyes. I see my mom and my brother so far away. I see myself at six years old, how I used to wear big round glasses, so quiet and shy. I feel a tinge of sadness stinging my throat, a tear rolls my cheek. So alone, so small, so sweet, so voiceless, so vulnerable.

My eyes burst wide open, and I gasp. Natalia hears my gasp, because now she's leaning close, and wiping the tears from my cheek. She whispers, "Are you ok?" I nod. We both settle back to our mats and close our eyes again.

Rosie is bathing the room with melodies from instruments I've never heard of. I'm on a mental and spiritual island, laying underneath a warm heavy rain shower. I wonder if this is what it feels like for religious people. The images in my mind are now swirls of reds and yellows and purples and blues. I'm on a whole other planet.

My skin tingles when I feel Natalia's fingertip touch mine. I feel the rush throughout my veins, that familiar high that I've gotten before around her. We're only touching the tips of our pinkies, and my entire body is exhilarated.

Rosie's closer to us now, so close that I can feel her standing directly above Natalia and me, just a foot away from our faces. She's swaying instruments directly above us, in my personal space. But I'm not bothered by it; I'm wanting more and more. The rush of sound flows into my pores. Natalia and I ride these escalating waves of sound together. She moves the tips of her fingers one single cell at a time, to meet mine. Her patience is building such an intense desire in me. I can feel the pouring raindrops' taps, and whooshes from the instruments dripping onto us. The wind chimes glide over us.

Natalia's hand has made it on top of mine now. *My skin is craving yours*, her fingertips tell me. We're communicating with only touch, and I respond back to her by sliding my fingers onto hers, careful not to break contact. With the slowest movements I've ever made, I trace the outline of her fingers, adding more pressure as I work my way up to her wrists. In our minds we're the only two people in this room.

The sounds are so all-consuming, I can feel my breath getting stronger. The muffled drums are pounding around us and creating a vibration in my bones. The warmth works its way down past my navel, building stronger and stronger. Our hands are now clasped tightly together as we hold on and don't dare let go.

Natalia and I float back down to earth, our bodies are held up by our mats, as I open my eyes and see people are back in the room with us. I can't believe this just happened. My entire body is so warm, my breath is recovering. Natalia brings my hand to her lips and kisses my index finger.

She's awoken a part of me that I never dared tap into. She's breathed life back into me.

We walk hand in hand to the grocery store parking lot.

"What else do you want to do in this little time we have here?" she asks.

"You mean tonight? I really should be getting home. It's late," I say, fumbling in my purse for my keys.

"No, I mean in this little time we have here on this planet. I'm sure you have dreams like everyone else. If you could do anything, besides being a therapist and a mom and a hot date," she says with a wink, "what would you want to do?"

"Oh, gosh. I never even have time to slow down to think about anything like that. The only thing I can think of is I used to keep a journal, but it's been a while since I've sat down to write anything. I'm always too tired and busy. Does that count?"

"It could be a start," she says.

"It was more like a Dear Diary type of thing, and then I'd write down my dreams sometimes." I feel a bit of nostalgia.

"Have you ever wanted to write a novel?"

"Oh wow, me?" I laugh. "All I've ever known myself to be is a therapist. That's my identity. Therapists write self-help books. Creative people write novels."

"Therapists can be creative," she says.

"Really?" She's got my wheels turning.

"You could start with writing down your dreams and then just see what happens from there."

"My dreams, ha. I don't even think like that anymore. I can hardly get through each day," I say.

"It seems like some important stuff came up for you during the sound bath," she cares enough to even notice. Although I don't want to talk about it.

"I don't want to talk about it," I say, and chew on the hangnail on my thumb.

"Ok, well when you're ready to talk about it, I won't have any expectations or give you unsolicited advice. I'll just listen."

"It's my dad," I blurt out.

She nods and we both know I'm going against what I said three seconds ago.

"He's been trying to contact me for years, like sending me letters, and texting me non-stop with pictures from my childhood. I just have no interest whatsoever to have him in my life."

We continue walking while she listens as promised.

"He feels like my stalker, and I feel angry that he doesn't move on with his life and leave me alone."

"Did he hurt you?" She asks.

"I don't know. No, he didn't. Well, not in the physical way. He didn't protect me from what my uncle did to me. He still let him come over for dinners and babysit me, even after he knew what his brother was doing."

"Have you ever told him why you're angry and why you don't respond to his messages?"

"I haven't. And he might not even have a clue as to why I don't pick up the phone."

"It sounds like he wasn't ready to be a dad, or just didn't know how to handle these kinds of things the right way. Maybe someday you can get real with him, for your own sake and having closure on that part of your childhood. I'm so sorry you went through that," she says as we reach my car.

Although we've just spent hours together, I'm disappointed we already have to say goodnight, which is opposite of my typical introvert style.

"I don't want to talk about the past. I want to savor this very moment. Tonight was pure magic. Thank you," I say to Natalia. She faces me and holds my waist, pressing me up against the car door.

"You deserve nothing less," she says. Her hands move strands of hair away from my face, and her eyes take me in. Our faces are close enough that I can smell her sweet lipstick, or maybe that's just in my imagination. Or maybe I'm imagining all of this. I smile at her, and follow what my heart tells me. Is this what love addiction feels like? Is this a fantasy? Every touch feels like I'm high on ecstasy, but hopefully without the hangover.

Her hand reaches up and behind my neck, cupping the back of my head, her fingertips in my hair, pressing into my scalp, pulling me towards her. I'm craving her taste, and my lips part a little. We're so close, I swear I'm inhaling her breath. She stays here in this space with me.

Time stands still.

A man whistles as he flies by us on a scooter. We both laugh a little and loosen our grip on one another. "Goodnight," I say.

"Goodnight, for now." She opens my car door for me. I get in and sigh deeply. She disappears into the night and I turn on Spotify. Sia's "Breathe Me" is cued up. I sing along with it as I drive back to the West Side: *"Be my friend, hold me, wrap me up, unfold me…"*

I graze my top lip with my index finger, imagining what it would feel like to finally kiss her. I feel alive.

Chapter Ten:

Drowning

Surfer's Park is crowded on this unusually chilly June morning. The Barbies and Kens of Santa Monica are walking advertisements, sporting Lululemon jackets and capris, and pushing their kids in Pottery Barn strollers. Couples are scattered around the park. Parents are in clusters by the playground, with their kids sprinkled everywhere, and a bootcamp group is doing their thing on a patch of grass facing the ocean.

Lily's walking between Dylan and me, with her hands in soft mittens clasping ours. We stop for a moment as Dylan squats down to face Lily and adjusts her jacket. He zips it all the way up so that her neck is covered, pulls the hoodie over her head and she points to her nose. "My little Lilykin, all bundled up and warm," he says in a playful voice as he gives her a kiss on her tiny nose as she instructed.

"Lily *King*, Daddy," she corrects him with a giggle. I smile as I watch them, and rub the outsides of my arms, an unsuccessful attempt to warm up my cold body.

"Hey, bro! You guys leaving?" Dylan asks a couple sitting on a wooden bench up ahead, who just uncoiled themselves from cuddles and are now zipping up their own kids' jackets.

"Yeah, it's all yours," one of the dads responds, pointing at the bench with his chin while he and his partner manage to buckle their kids into a massive double stroller.

"Thanks, man," Dylan says. He pats the guy on his shoulder and they already seem like old friends.

I see a group of teenage girls on the wooden bench near us, adorned by manicured palm trees, with non-fat lattes in hand and trendy scarves snuggled around their necks. They carry on what I imagine are gossipy conversations—*Popular Teen Social Requirements 101*. I feel the familiar nausea in the pit of my stomach and a sting in my chest when I remember the social cliques back in high school. My throat closes up, my palms are clammy and my feet are cemented into the ground. I wonder if social anxiety ever truly goes away. Thank God it's nothing like it used to be every day in high school, but these small panic attacks still suck. I can treat patients all day long and help them regulate their moods with anxiety reduction techniques, yet it seems nearly impossible to apply any of that to my own life. My patients are a hell of a lot braver than I am.

My eyes are burning, and I can't tell if it's from the bright sunlight, a new symptom of anxiety that just graced me with its presence, or just the usual insufficient sleep of a working mom. I hear music in the distance, and it gets louder as I turn to see a Surfer's Park golf cart pull over to the side of the bike path. It's beach chic, has a cobalt blue body with thin white orchid decals, a teak wooden bench, and an extended compartment with a mobile espresso bar and a display of snacks and merchandise for sale.

The tall college kid driving it steps out in a white polo shirt with *SM Local* embroidered in cursive across the back, and green plaid knee-length shorts. Through blue lensed aviator sunglasses, Local is cool as a cucumber while tending to the swarm of kids and parents needing their suntan lotion, overpriced water, and latte refills. I don't miss those days, I say to myself, remembering one of my first jobs as a golf cart girl in college selling high-priced beer to men who thought they were slick, telling stupid jokes I had to pretend were funny.

Lily still hasn't graduated from the swings to the climbing structures like her peers. So here I am, pushing her as she flies into the air, giving me orders. "Mommy, look!" She's too timid to attempt climbing onto the giant surfboard apparatus in the center of the park with all the other kids. She won't speak to a single person besides Dylan or me.

A 30 something-year-old couple is sitting at one of the picnic tables made of vintage surfboards in the large grassy area. They're in their own little world, and can't get enough of each other. What ever happened to those days? Once they're gone, it seems like they're permanently embedded in the pre-marriage chapters with no chance for resurfacing later on in the love story. Or maybe there is...

I look over at Dylan, who's across the playground, standing in the middle of a group of parents. He's in his element. He's charming, funny, charismatic, pulling in everyone's attention as he delivers one of his many stories in the most alluring way. Not one person has their eyes anywhere else but on him. This is the guy I fell in love with, the same way I'm watching his groupies are too. He's the star of the show and his audience has no idea I'm his passive investor.

Lily's over the swings by now. She jumps off and we step onto the walkway, taking our time heading towards the *SM Local* crowd, which has calmed down by now. I like her timing. It helps with my social anxiety that still rears its ugly head now and again.

"What do people do all day if they don't work?" Lily asks me, her eyes are on the people around us.

I look across the playground. Dylan's animated and acting out an apparently mind-blowing story, surrounding him with the laughter and giddy looks from his captive audience.

"Well, I don't know. That's a very good question. What do you think they do all day?" I look over at Dylan.

He's not the same man I married. Or is he?

He's still the attractive, charming, attentive go-getter I met in college. He's the same guy who planned a breathtaking romantic surprise proposal in his parent's gorgeous backyard in front of everyone we know. That's who I'm looking at right now.

But in another breath, I'm seething in silent rage. I stare at him and my blood boils as I think about how none of these people have any idea what's behind the curtain. They have no idea who pays for the roof over his head while he's on the computer all day doing

God knows what in his pajamas, getting drunk, eating and taking up all the space in our lives, while I work like a slave for him, disappear from burn-out, invisibility and lack of appreciation.

It's been months since Dylan and I have had sex. I can't even remember the last time we kissed, other than obligatory pecks when I leave for or arrive from work. The world feels like it's spinning. All these days are rolling into one. I just can't seem to come up for air. My sessions are back to back, and I can't afford to take a break because Dylan still hasn't found a job. He gets defensive every time I ask if he's even applied or has any interviews. His favorite line is, "Don't worry about it. I'll figure it out."

It's so frustrating because when I met him we were both were on track to have solid careers so that we could be financially independent. I remember that before we were married, I was so proud of myself for saving $20,000 in my bank account. It was the first time in my life that I had ever seen that many zeros in my account. It was something that hadn't come easily. I had diligently assigned ten percent of every single paycheck to savings. I made my lunches during the week, and set aside specific cash for spending money on the weekends.

I ran every morning back then, rain or shine, even if it was just for ten minutes. That was my religion. It was my refueling time, the time that was solely for me to be outside and clear my mind, to recharge and nourish my body, to go for as long or as little as I felt like running. I had figured out the way I preferred to eat, and what foods I wanted to buy from the market. I no longer lived on autopilot, and started making different choices than the way I was raised. I stuck to the outside edges of the market where all the fresh produce and natural foods were, and never set foot in the center of the store where the processed foods were. I felt balanced spiritually, mentally, financially, and physically. Cut to years later and life feels so overwhelming now and I'm losing myself. I don't even know which way is up and I can't breathe. I feel suffocated and exhausted, and have absolutely not one single minute to even think or recharge.

Weekends don't really feel like weekends anymore. What happened to sleeping in, and lunches with friends where I didn't even pay attention to what time it was? What happened to being taken care of by Dylan, like at the beginning of the relationship? I feel like he has incredible marketing skills. He planned and paid for and took care of everything at the beginning. He wined and dined me, and treated me like a queen.

He massaged me and touched me, and felt like he really took me in. He pleasured me, and was attentive and cared enough to be patient and take his time until he knew I reached orgasm. He would kiss me slowly, and focus on giving to me.

When he drank, it was more than everyone else, but he never got sick. He never got out of control. It annoyed me, but it wasn't something that impacted us much. In hindsight, I should have known. He would hang out with his friends until six in the morning! I would be getting up and ready for work, and he'd come to my place and bring me breakfast at the end of his late-night hangout. I thought it was a little odd, but was so overtaken by his charm, and by him so generously taking care of me in the morning, that I was too distracted to see how his lifestyle was nothing close to mine.

Now, everything is the opposite. I'm exhausted every single waking moment. I don't remember the last time I felt rested. I have panic attacks at least weekly. It's out of control. It's been forever since we've had any pleasure between us. The last time was probably the night we got married. I swear, that's the last time I can remember. The only pleasuring that happens now is him receiving it. In every which way. Whether I'm housing him, massaging him, pleasuring him until he reaches orgasm…it's all about him, and he's completely fine with receiving and taking. I just don't understand how someone could change so much after getting married. He's an entirely different person.

"Your hands are wet." Lily reminds me that despite the crisp winter temperature this Saturday morning, I can't hide my feelings.

"That happens to me sometimes," I tell her, as I jolt out of the mental spiral I was in for the last several minutes. Lily's now curled into her standard position: velcroed to my leg, head down, frown across her brow. I kiss her on the top of her head. It's our turn to order at the SM Local golf cart. I'm jealous and astounded by Local's calm demeanor. After the huge crowd of demanding patrons, Local is unfazed and you'd think Lily and I were the first customers of the day.

Lily cradles her hot chocolate as we walk away from the cart and onto the pathway leading back to the playground. "Thank you, Mommy." I can see a tiny spark in her personality; it's dim, but it's there. I know it. I feel it. I have no idea if she's ever going to break out of this shy, mute phase, but I pray she does. It would kill me if she lived her life as muzzled as I have.

"Graaarrr!" Dylan has somehow managed to sneak up behind us. He pinches me on the butt, no matter how many times I've told him that it hurts and I hate it! He scoops Lily into his arms. Her hot chocolate spills a little, but she doesn't care, as she's giggling and squealing with delight.

I hate that I love him right now. Love is a prickly blanket.

Chapter Eleven:

Sketches

I wake up to the most thrilling sensation. Natalia's hands are massaging my neck and shoulders. My entire body is warm. She's taking her time, and taking me in. The ocean breeze from our Malibu hotel room is perfectly warm. She's holding me as if she's worshipping every inch of me. She makes me feel like I'm the most beautiful woman in the world.

Our hearts are pounding in unison, and I can feel the rush inside me getting stronger and stronger. "I like this so much," I whisper to her.

"What?" Dylan asks.

"Hmm?" I open my eyes, disoriented and startled.

"You were talking in your sleep again. At least you weren't sleepwalking," he says in that you're-such-an-idiot tone I hate.

I come to and realize where my fingers are and I couldn't be more obvious. I was so close to reaching orgasm, I had to have been loud. Did he even notice?

His loud snores give me my answer.

I pull out my phone. My fingers press and slide across the screen until her name shows up, and quickly type three words.

Me: I miss you

I can't believe I sent that. The butterflies in my stomach are fluttering around my entire body now. I delete the entire conversation, close my eyes again and try with all my might to step back into that dream.

*   *   *   *

The house still isn't ready, and everyone's supposed to be arriving at any moment. Time has been a point of contention with Dylan and me over the years. In his world, the start time of an event translates to the time you leave the house, which means with LA traffic plus finding parking, we're at least 45 minutes late for everything. Tonight we're hosting game night at our place, and I can already envision him still mopping the floors as our friends arrive.

I'm wiping down the kitchen counters when I hear a thunk from another room.

"I'm ok!" Lily calls out.

"Ok!" I shout back. She's just too freakin' cute.

I step out of the kitchen and pass Dylan, who's in his usual spot on the couch. Lily's coloring; she puts down her pencil and meets me in the bathroom, and I start working on her hair.

I'm going through my mental checklist before everyone gets here. The only other thing I asked Dylan to do besides mop the floors this morning was to set a platter of hors d'oeuvres on the table right before the guests arrive. I decided on easy and delicious: stuffed mushrooms and deviled eggs. The recipes said they should take about twenty minutes from prep to completion, but since Dylan is in charge of setting those out tonight, we can double that time. I'm brushing Lily's hair and can hear commotion in the kitchen. I assume Dylan's perfectionism is in full gear, and I hear him groaning and cursing, confirming that he's started the hors d'oeuvres all over again because something just wasn't right. I do have to give him credit. When I give him a list of things to do, he gets them done. It takes him forever and a day, and he often redoes my own work which annoys the heck out of me, but he'll do them and do them well. I'd put money on those hors d'oeuvres being camera ready and delicious enough for a cooking show. I just wish I wasn't the manager of our household and required to dictate to everyone what to do, make sure we're on time, and to repeat myself over and over again.

"Babe, did you mop the floors yet?" I yell from the bathroom. I should know better than this. I need to not be so hard on him, and I need to let go of my own control and perfectionism, as shouting will only escalate things. I asked him to do it right after we woke up this morning, while I cleaned the kitchen, the bathrooms, and took Lily to the market with me. At the time, he told me not to worry, and that he'd handle it. Twelve hours later, I'm certain the mop is still in the garage bone dry.

"I'm doing it right now! I said don't worry about it!" he shouts back.

I roll my eyes and let out a heavy sigh. God, I hate when he talks to me like that. He uses this tone that basically says, "You're such an idiot for asking me anything." Why do these little things get under my skin? It's just the floors. Who cares? He means well and he does eventually get to them. Maybe I'm just an overly critical, nagging wife. Maybe I'm too sensitive. I know he's intense, and maybe it's just the way he talks. I know he's a good guy.

"Mommy, can we play Sketches tonight?" Lily knows our game night protocol by now. Or is this her attempt at deflection? I'm sure she senses the thick tension in the air.

"Of course, sweetheart," I say. "When I'm finished with your hair, you can set it up on the coffee table for you and the twins, and put the playing cards and poker chip case on the dining room table for the big kids." I kiss the back of her head, and finish brushing her hair. She's facing the mirror and looking at me in the reflection, playing with Max on the bathroom sink. She tugs and wiggles his ears, and swings his arms up and down, letting him dance with her. I love watching her get entranced in imaginary play. It's so sweet and innocent. Did she hear my sigh over all the commotion? I need to watch that. I just can't believe I let our tension splash onto her.

I set the brush down, and gather three chunks of her hair with my fingers to start her French braid. Her silky thick blonde hair wants to slip out of my hands, but I've learned by now to keep a firm grip and twist it close to her scalp so the braid is tight. I've practiced this on her in more ways than I've ever done on my own hair. I keep pulling more strands of hair, twisting, pulling, twisting and pulling, until I get to the very bottom and secure it with a hairband on the end.

"Do you need to use the restroom one more time?" I ask her. It's my own PTSD response after countless accidents. It doesn't happen nearly as often as it used to, but it still does every once in a while. She's going to be five soon and I know from my line of work that patients who are over five years old, still wetting themselves, and don't have any medical conditions are often diagnosed with enuresis, which means that if they're old enough to be toilet trained, even someone who didn't attend grad school for psychology would guess it to be a strong sign of emotional distress. This just isn't ok. I don't know what else to do. I've taken her to the doctor, and tried every trick in the book.

As I'm standing behind her and we're both looking at her hair in the reflection of the mirror, I notice the strange sensation that my feet feel wet and I look down. The carpet underneath Lily and me is soaked.

"*Are you serious?!*" The words explode out of me and I throw the brush against the wall. A chip of paint falls off.

Lily gasps and starts softly whimpering.

I've reached my limit and can't take it anymore. I'm in a mental spiral, which has been all too common over the last couple years.

"*What's going on?!*" Dylan yells from the kitchen.

"Nothing! It's fine." I lie. The last thing I need right now is to have him upset over this. I'll never hear the end of it.

Lily's soft whimpers have turned into inconsolable crying, and she's hyperventilating. "I wasn't built for this!"

I close my eyes and take a few deep breaths. I need to try to regain some sort of sanity and dignity, if there is even any left at this point. I turn to Lily who is standing in soaked clothes with pee down her legs and looking at the puddle on the carpet. She hasn't moved an inch. She's having a panic attack. God! How did we get here? How is this even happening? How is my little girl so scared and sad? How has this become our life? Why am I making such a big deal over a simple accident?

I bend to her eye level and look at her little face, and slowly all of my anger and frustration melt off me and the guilt creeps in. I hold her close, not caring that now we are both soaked in her pee.

"It's ok," I keep repeating to her. "Breathe," I pull back after a few moments and wipe away her tears, kissing her forehead.   Her breathing has calmed down.

"I'm so sorry," I say to her. "You're not in trouble. I got mad and upset and I shouldn't have thrown the brush and scared you like that. You didn't do anything wrong, ok?" She looks up at me and her panic and her breathing gradually slow down.

She nods softly.

I'm a horrible mom.

"Let's clean up and then you can pick out which ribbon you want for your hair." I pick up Max from the floor, who had fallen from her arms during my tantrum and turn on the shower.

*   *   *   *

That detour felt like hours.   But here we are. We've survived my flip out, everyone's refreshed and most importantly - dry.   I put the brush and container of hair bands away in a drawer, and wipe away the paint chips that had dropped onto the counter.

Even though it's my friends who are coming over, and I've know Dylan's friends for years—I still feel a burning sensation inside my chest. My social anxiety was born when I was Lily's age, and hasn't left my life since. "Here we go," I whisper to myself, and sigh deeply.

As I'm heading to the dining area, I'm shocked to see Dylan's set out the hors d'oeuvres in a colorful display on our wooden dining table between two large vases of fresh flowers I got from the market this morning. Helen and Sarah texted me earlier that they're bringing wine and dessert, and Jake and Jane are bringing lasagna. I can smell the hors d'oeuvres staying warm in the kitchen.

Dylan's glass of whiskey is sitting on the counter, fresh and it looks like he's a few sips in. I roll my eyes. I really don't feel like smelling vomit in our bathroom in the morning. He couldn't be any more different from me, my lifestyle, my temperament. Ugh, why am I so uptight? Who cares if he drinks a little? I just pray he doesn't take it over the edge tonight. Who am I kidding? Of course he will.

Lily is sitting on the sofa opening up her Sketches game.

Shockingly, the floors are mopped, but of course they're soaking wet because Dylan just finished; I can hear him rolling the mop bucket back into the garage. But no one's here yet. So it shouldn't matter anyway. I'm too hard on him.

The doorbell chimes. "Or maybe I'm not," I whisper to myself, and my *Empathy For Dylan Moment* has come and gone. Lily hops off the sofa, runs to me and clings to my leg. She's returned to turtle mode.

I hold onto her shoulder so I can maintain my balance as I walk to the front door, pulling it open with my free hand.

"Kyle!" Even though he's eight inches taller than me, he'll always be my adorable little brother. He softens the energy in the air instantly.

"Hey sister, I missed ya at dinner the other night. Mom wants you to call her." He gives me a hug, then squats like a frog down to Lily. "Ribbit, Lily, Ribbit." He manages to get a tiny giggle out of her, but she doesn't dare detach herself from my leg. He's patient, and knows it's only a matter of time until she'll warm up. He stands back up and holds out a bottle of Merlot for me to look at, before pulling it back towards his chest. He thrusts it toward me again, I move to grab it and he pulls it back again. "I know you don't drink anything but water and tea. I'll go put this in the fridge to chill." He puts one hand on my shoulder to nudge me aside, and walks past Lily and me.

I see Helen crossing our quiet street toward the house. "Helen! I'm glad you made it!" I say, dipping into autopilot hostess mode. She's gorgeous as always, walking up my driveway in a yellow dress flowing to just below her knees, and white strappy heels. She leans in to give me an armless hug, as her hands are occupied—bright yellow orchids in one and a foil-wrapped dish in the other.

"Where's Sarah? I thought you guys were coming together," I say as I take the flowers.

"She texted me and said she's getting a ride from this attorney guy; I think his name's Luke."

"Why does she have an attorney?" I ask naïvely.

"Jelina, seriously?" Helen purses her lips, bewildered that I still just don't get these hints.

"Maybe someday I'll understand her wild and free sex life," I say and gasp and cover my face with my hand, as I catch myself saying that in front of Lily. I try to change the subject. "Thank you for these gorgeous orchids!"

"I got them at Trader Joe's, and the cake at SM Cucina, of course," she says as she heads for the kitchen. "Where do you want me to set this down?"

"Don't go in the kitchen! The floors are still wet," I shout as she reaches the doorway, and my annoyance at Dylan's procrastination covers me like an oily film on my skin.

"Helen, what's up?" Dylan swoops around her and pulls her into a suave dancing motion with him, sweeping her off her feet. Before she can respond, she's giggling and so lost in his charm that she doesn't even realize he's taken her dish. "Damn! Someone's a chef!" He holds the dish up to his face, peeling back the foil and peeking at it, closes his eyes for a moment and breathes it in. "A chocolate lava cake! I hope you guys enjoy everything else we're having, because this is all I'm having tonight." He disappears with the dessert.

Helen's blushing. Are you kidding me? She's actually blushing. How does he do it? He can pull anyone in with a few seconds of his charm. I soften a bit.

"Good to see you too, D!" she yells, gathering her composure and possibly coming out of his spell and back to remembering how I've vented about him so many times before. She turns and comes over to

Lily, who's let go of my leg by now, and was lost in joy for a moment, laughing at the entertaining Dylan and Helen dance show she just witnessed. She loves her daddy so much. I'm grateful for it. It's one of those things I love about him. I can never take that away from her. "Lily, I heard you wrote a cool book for Miss Kayla's class! Can I see it?" Helen extends her hand, which is left hanging.

Lily's expression turns from a big smile back to looking down at the floor. Her frown returns and she chews on a fingernail. She sits on the couch, fiddling with her Sketches and doesn't say a word.

Helen knows it's not a time to push. She'll warm up in about an hour—or maybe not.

The doorbell rings. That must be Sarah and her new "friend." Oh dear, this woman. I can't keep track of all her men. But out of all of us, she's enjoying her life the most and is happier than anyone.

"I'll get it!" Dylan says. I see him re-enter the room and fly towards the door. "Hey, you guys are early!" It's Jake and Jane and their twins. He's right. They're usually on Dylan's timeline ever since they had kids. Their daughters are a couple of years older than Lily, but they couldn't be more different from her.

Sarah is walking up the driveway with her flavor of the month. "Sarah! Hey, come on in!" Dylan shouts. "And who's this lucky guy?" They all pour into the house, and the volume and energy goes up about ten notches. I can feel my body tense as my introversion is starting to feel the pressure.

"This is Luke," Sarah says, motioning to her date. "Luke, Dylan. Dylan, Luke." She glides past them and straight to me. "Jelina, meet my friend, Luke."

I can't keep my eyes off him. I'm too nervous to get any words out. I'm surprised by this one. He doesn't look like her typical tattooed personal trainer type. Luke's dressed in cream-colored slacks and a button-down shirt fitted to his athletic body, with the sleeves rolled up to expose his tan skin and muscular forearms. He has a nicely trimmed goatee and blue-lensed aviator sunglasses resting on his head. This guy's got to be out on the Malibu hiking trails every weekend, and I get confirmation when I catch the natural highlights in his wavy hair. He seems comfortable to be around. He extends his hand to Dylan. "It's a pleasure to meet you, Dylan." They shake hands, and he steps back and waits for Sarah to enter the house first, putting his hand on her lower back.

Why is my heart beating faster? My hands are sweaty, and I'm embarrassed. This never happens when I meet one of Sarah's guys. And I love my husband. Don't I? I do! Yes, of course I do. I hate him sometimes, but he's still my husband. I just wish he would treat me with this much class. I wish he would be considerate of me.

"Jelina! I'm going to find a bottle opener" Sarah says, heading to the kitchen with her Pinot Noir. I hope Dylan didn't catch my teenage crush moment. It would kill me if he saw that, and I hurt his feelings. Sarah gives me a kiss on the cheek and does the same to Helen. "Let the games begin!" she shouts, holding the wine she brought high in the air and taking Helen's hand, who grabs mine as they fly into the kitchen. I almost drop the orchids when Lily bumps my arm, catching up and following behind our train as our little caboose. I give up on making sure the floors are dry. If we slip, we slip.

The house is filled with color and life. My anxiety is lingering, as I'm soaking everything in: the muffled conversations in other rooms, the smells of hors d'oeuvres mixing with everyone's colognes and perfumes and shampoos, the guys' deep voices filling the dining room, and I see Luke and Kyle accepting an invitation to share the new whiskey Dylan wants them to try. The twins are running around. The soundtrack to their existence consists of vacillating between laughing, screaming, and singing, and it all blends in with the background of light jazz music I put on earlier—all while their parents are hiding out in the backyard getting high for a few minutes. It still amazes me that grown adults feel the need to do this. They come over, put the lasagna on the table, and immediately go to the backyard to get high before doing anything. Interesting.

I guess I'm such a control freak, I'll never understand purposefully doing something to take away my control. Why on earth would anyone want to volunteer to lose control? When I think about my patients, and what's led a lot of them to alcohol and drug addiction, it makes sense. But when it's so close to home, and with my friends, sometimes we're too close to the words to be able to read the story clearly. They walk back in and join Dylan and Luke. Dylan's playing bartender and pouring glasses of whiskey. I can see their bloodshot eyes from all the way over here, and they're lounging on our chairs like they're on vacation for a couple weeks.

Ah, now I get it. The only thing I can relate this to is love and sex. That's my high and my escape. It gives me the same euphoria that I see on their faces right now. They don't have a care in the world. The ear-piercing screams of their girls, the energy of them running around the house—it's all faded into the background as if they're both wearing headphones: euphoria with a Bob Marley playlist. I can read on their faces that they're grateful that at least their kids are contained within four walls and possibly have a bunch of other adults to share in the parental responsibilities for a few hours tonight.

Lily has decided against playing with her peers, and is still trailing behind me like my mini shadow as I chat in the kitchen with Helen and Sarah. I don't blame her. I know she gets excited to see them before they arrive, but those twins are exhausting to even be around, and their parents are in no hurry to spend an ounce of energy taming them. I'm not either, for that matter. Lily will gravitate towards them at her own pace, and when they've tired themselves out a bit. I put my arm around her and she nuzzles into me and holds onto my leg.

"So, your attorney seems… sweet," I say to Sarah.

"Well, that he is," she replies with a wink. She takes three glasses from the cupboard, and sets them on the granite countertop. Helen is in sync with her, already opening the Pinot Noir.

"Sarah…" I say, giving her a look. She knows I don't drink.

"Jelina…" she comes over and squeezes me in a tight hug, which is now a group hug with my orchids and Lily, who's still holding onto my leg. "You know I like teasing you. And what's one little sip going to do? Come on, it won't hurt to loosen up a bit."

"Aww, you guys are adorable," Helen says, pouring Pinot into all three glasses. She knows they'll both finish whatever I don't drink.

I love these girls, but my introversion kicks in with too much physical touch, and right now all my senses are in overdrive. I break free and set the orchids down in the middle of the counter. Sarah helps Lily up onto a barstool, playing with her braid as Lily caresses the soft yellow orchid leaves. She's simply precious. I open the fridge and pull out the fruit and cheese platters.

"So, how did it happen?" Helen asks. "You just walk into his office to hire him for representation, and instead of paying a retainer, he asks you out on a date?"

"A lady never tells." Sarah sashays back to the counter, grabbing two glasses and handing one to me.

"So, pretty much," Helen says and shakes her head. "Unbelievable. And look at him! He's even more perfect than the last one."

I set the platter on the counter and remove the plastic wrap. Helen gets stack of plates from the cupboard and sets them down on the table near the silverware.

"You girls are having the time of your lives. I'm happy for you, really," I say, but I'm lying through my teeth, holding in my envy. Fine, I'm happy for them, but God! I'm so jealous of their freedom. Their lives are fun. I can't remember the last time I would have described my life as "fun"—if ever. We signed up for such different lives, different lifestyles. I signed up for the one I was "supposed" to live. I never once slowed down long enough to even question if it was what I truly wanted, what would truly make me happy. I make a plate of hors d'oeuvres and fruit for Lily, look down at her, and hang my arm over her shoulder. "Hey, what do you think about helping me with Sketches?" Her face lights up, and she nods. It's her favorite board game.

Helen is cutting slices of lasagna, and Sarah is passing around the plates of fruit and cheese and hors d'oeuvres. I stack two plates with food for Lily and me and float with her to the living room. We settle onto the oversized shag rug that stretches from the sofa, holds up the coffee table and sprawls for several feet beyond. I let my toes and the sides of my feet take comfort in the thick cotton fibers. Much better. So cozy. I can breathe now. I look over at Lily. She feels it too, I know it. I'm always more comfortable around people outside of my age group than my own peers in these crowded situations. I guess I can relate to Lily in this way.

The twins bounce over and land on the sofa. They're leaning over the coffee table, grabbing at the Sketches box as I'm pulling the lid off.

"Ok girls! Hold on, hold on!" Thank God I only have one, and she's a mellow one. "You're all going to get a chance to play, I promise. We just have to get it all out of the box first. Here." I hand the twins a deck of cards split in half. "You two are going to be in charge of shuffling these." I turn to Lily. "And you, my dear, are going to make sure everyone has a notepad, a pencil, and put the dice in the middle. I'll be the timekeeper. Remember, when it's your turn to pull the card, only say the Clue aloud, and read the Sketch to yourself." I hear the adults gathering around the dining room table, and the poker chips being distributed.

"Babe, what the hell are you doing on the floor at the kids' table? Get over here!" Dylan yells. God! His tone is like nails on a chalkboard. Even his invitations sound like he can't stand me. I feel my face turn red from humiliation when everyone laughs awkwardly.

"Maybe later." I force the words out. More like never. The last thing I want to do is move from this spot. He has a way of making me feel like the stupidest person on the planet in two seconds flat. Congratulations, Dylan. Mission accomplished. I officially want to disappear. My need to be invisible is so strong right now.

All the sounds in the house are muffled, and I feel like I've just slipped into a pool and my ears are clogged. My heart's beating out of my chest and I feel so cold, I'm shaking. Everything's blurry, and I can't maintain focus. I'm trying hard to see what's in front of me and the only thing I can make out is a bright glowing object at the end of the sofa. It's the little girl! She's sitting there, writing in her notebook. I'm paralyzed when it all hits me. She's *me* as a little girl! I knew she felt familiar when I saw her that night in the kitchen. I feel a deep love for that little girl as I see her in my mind's eye. I feel a deep longing to hold her and protect her. I want so badly to go towards her and hold her and talk to her and get to know her, but my legs won't move, my mouth won't open.

I feel my phone vibrate in my pocket. I pull it out, and when I look up again, the girl has completely disappeared, and no one else even noticed that she was here a moment ago.

My phone continues to buzz. I click it open. I have 13 new messages?!! Not now. Why won't he just leave me alone?

My fingers do the very opposite of what my mind and heart want. They go right ahead and click that stupid notification. What's happening is exactly what I feared: countless texts and they won't stop.

Dad: Be strong and courageous; do not be frightened or dismayed, for the Lord your God is with you wherever you go - Joshua 1:9

I sought the Lord, and he answered me, and delivered me from all my fears - Psalm 34:4

Cast all your anxiety on him because he cares for you - Peter 5:7

He gives power to the weak and strength to the powerless - Isaiah 40:29

"Ugh!" I say out loud, startling the twins, which I thought was impossible. "Sorry, guys. My phone is just acting up." I toss it onto the rug.

While I was in La-La Land, Lily and the twins are well into the game. "My turn!" one of them shouts, and rolls the dice. I pick my phone back up and continue reading the texts.

> Dad: I'm sorry
> I want to talk.
> 555-0180
> Please call me
> I love you

I'm stunned. He's never actually written to me like having a normal conversation. My palms are sweating and my heart hasn't resumed beating yet.

> Dad: I left you all alone
> Those things should never happen to a little girl
> I didn't protect you
> I didn't listen to you
> I didn't believe you
> I'm sorry

I wipe a tear from my cheek, and keep scrolling.

> Dad: Are you there?
> J?

I can feel you

I take a breath.

Dad: I'm so sorry
Please call me

I wipe more tears away. I look around and I'm surprised the kids haven't noticed me crying, but they're too involved in their game.

My fingers have a mind of their own and are actually typing back to him.

Me: I do—

I delete those three little letters, turn off my phone and set it on the floor. My back stretches and overextends my posture. I see Lily rolling the dice, and I scoot closer to her.

Lily counts her dice. "Six, seven, eight."

One of the twins pulls eight cards from the stack in the center of the table, and hands the last one to Lily. She takes it and reads her clue to herself. I peek over at her clue, which isn't that hard because she's not hiding it very well. *If You Had A Magic Wand, What Would You Make With It?*

"Mom, don't look," she whispers to me. Even though she's painfully shy, she still calls me out on peeking at her card. She's so cute, I can't take it sometimes. She's very serious about this game.

"Oh yes! Of course," I say, just as serious. I flip the timer over.

She takes her pencil between her little fingers and starts her sketch quickly. The twins are leaning over and getting riled up, even blocking Lily's line of sight as she's drawing. "C'mon, give the artist some room here," I say, waving my hands as to shoo them away.

Lily's tongue is doing that thing it does when she's lost in concentration with her homework. I can hardly make out what she's drawing, but I just love that she's trying anyway and at least she's drawing with them instead of being frozen stuck to my leg. Then, she's done.

And just like one of those autostereogram paintings I have in my office where you stare at it until the picture pops out at you like it's in 3-D, Lily's drawing does just that! It's incredible..

One of the twins yells in my ear, "Time!" Point taken, kid. I'm the world's worst timekeeper.

"Ok, who wants to guess first?" I ask the small crowd.

The twins don't even wait.

"A mountain!"

"A swamp!

"No," Lily peeps, and I can see she's embarrassed and is getting that look on her face where she wants to disappear and be mute for the rest of the night.

"It's a magical island," I say.

The color comes back to her face. "It is!"

"I see it! Here's the grass, and here are the little huts where people do fun things, and here's the ocean water where the girl is on a paddle-board."

"Oh!" the twins say in unison. "Ok, cool. My turn!" one of them says, grabbing the dice, clearly not as impressed as I am.

"I see it. It's beautiful, honey," I say to Lily and kiss her on the head. "Let's keep this one."

Chapter Twelve:

Roller Coaster

It's another cool morning, but my office usually feels snug during these group therapy days. I risk opening the sliding glass door to let some cool ocean air in. If the fire trucks outside start wailing their sirens, then so be it. I think I'll let Jack Johnson continue playing on my laptop speakers for a few minutes. He can help me welcome everyone in today.

The regulars are shuffling into their safe haven one at a time. It's so sweet that they each have their preferred spots. I took over this group last month when my colleague went on maternity leave, and I already love them like they're my kids; each precious in their own way.

Melissa's mascara is smudged, and I can't tell whether it's from exhaustion or crying this time. My guess is both, but she's getting stronger day by day. Somehow, she manages to make it into this room every week, and I can see her walking through her feelings in healthier ways. Eddie's wearing his usual scowl, accessorized by dark-lensed Ray-Bans and a lowered baseball cap. I wavered a bit on his first day, trying to decide whether or not to set a hard and fast "No Sunglasses or Hats During Groups" rule, but opted to let him bring down his walls at his own pace.

I can see he's brought back the copy of The Power of Vulnerability that I lent him from my bookshelf last week. Melissa notices too.

"Was it any good?" She asks, as she never gets tired of making the effort to connect with him, and she's a diehard Brené Brown fan, so I know she's genuinely curious if it moved him as much as it did her. I have to hand it to her. She really gets him. I think he's an external representation of her internal state.

It's endearing to watch their interactions. You'd think this 57-year-old man was 17 by the looks of him right now. He pulls on the lid of his baseball cap and lowers it even more. I smile, sitting back and observing them. What they don't realize is that even though it's not nine a.m. yet, group has already begun. The group dynamic is ever-present.

I can see Melissa is tempted to grab the book, but is trying very hard to apply the boundaries I called her out on last week. She respects his physical space but tries to connect again. "I love that part where Brené compares shame to the zoom lens on a camera, and how shame loses its power when it's said out loud." With that, he acknowledges her with a side-eye.

Moments later, Charlie walks in, carrying several hula hoops in his arms. "Well, good morning to all you lovely people! Looks like it's just us today." He nudges the door shut with his elbow. Melissa's cheeks turn as red as a tomato watching his grand entrance. I think she gets more passion from Charlie entering the room than she's gotten in her entire marriage.

"I read that new book you told me about. I loved how she basically wrote the book for me about my procrastination! And the part about boundaries gave me this idea," he announces, as he hands me a hula hoop.

"You mean Run For Your Mind, Write For Your Life?" I double check.

"Yeah," he says, as Melissa and Eddie take their hula hoops with confused expressions.

"We'll use these today when we listen to each other," Charlie continues. "This will be our Protection Boundary and...what's the other one?"

"Containment," I help him out.

"Yes, of course! The Containment Boundary," Charlie continues. "So no matter what other people think or feel, that stays outside of the hula hoop, and your own opinions and feelings are protected inside the hula hoop."

"For crying out loud," Eddie huffs.

Side-talk warms up the space between the walls. My eyes wander to the second hand on the clock by the window, and follow it as it patiently dances to the highest point.

I lower the laptop's volume slowly down to *Off*. The room adjusts to whispers, until the familiar comforting quiet emerges.

"Alright, everyone. Good morning, let's go ahead and start group. Welcome back to the Raw Room. You guys know the drill. Everything that's said here stays here in this room and is confidential, unless there's risk of harm to self or others—"

"Or dependent adults or kids," Charlie finishes for me.

"Thanks, Charlie," I say.

"Alright, raw and uncensored. Here we go. Let's get vulnerable, guys. Remember, respect is our only rule." I open the floodgates and let them start swimming.

"I'm up for trying out the hula hoops if you guys are," Melissa offers.

To everyone's surprise, Eddie pulls the hula hoop over his head along with the rest of us. We're all in this thing together.

"Really?" I joke with him.

"Why the hell not, huh?" He takes off his sunglasses and adjusts the hula hoop sitting around his waist. I love this guy.

There's a rhythm to these mornings and we find ourselves flowing with its cadence.

"I'm tired!" Melissa jumps right in. "I'm in a sexless marriage, I've lost all attraction to him, and I hate to say it but I both love *and* despise being a mom. I don't even know who I am anymore. If it wasn't for my kid, I'd kill myself." She looks at me, "Don't worry, I'm not gonna do it."

I nod, acknowledging that I heard her.

"Why not just leave if you're so unhappy?" Charlie snaps at her. The mood's shifted in the room. Both he and Eddie are looking annoyed. I imagine they're thinking about their own imaginary marriages.

"This is a good chance to practice those Protection and Containment Boundaries," I say, motioning to the hula hoop. "Remember to be curious about what Melissa is saying, and that everyone has a right to their own thoughts, even if you don't agree."

"It's not that simple," Melissa blurts out. "And I don't even want to," she says.

I draw her back towards herself, "Melissa, you said that if it weren't for your child, you'd kill yourself?"

"I wouldn't really. It's just a thought that crosses my mind sometimes," she says.

"Let's slow this down and explore it from a different angle. Now really think about this. What parts of the struggle do you wish you could kill off?" I ask her.

"I don't know," she pauses for a moment. "Like all the pressure I guess, having to do everything for everyone and have nothing left for myself," she says.

"That's a good start. Let's free yourself from those parts," I say.

I lean forward, letting my hula hoop drop to the ground. "We're going to try an inner child exercise."

The group members put their hula hoops off to the side and scoot their chairs in for a tighter circle.

"Take a breath, Melissa. How old are you feeling right now?" I ask.

"What do you mean? I'm 29."

"I want you to take your attention from here," I point to my head, "to here." I point to my heart. "Notice the feelings you're having, and float back to the first time you remember feeling this way."

Melissa closes her eyes and takes a deep inhale. After some time she says, "14."

"14, ok. Can you tell me about 'fourteen-year-old Melissa'?"

"She's staying up late for hours and hours doing AP Calculus homework."

"What's she like? Can you see the expression on her face?" I ask.

My office is silent, and it feels like we're all traveling back in time with her.

"Tired, always tired. And angry. I remember mom telling me to smile more. I hated that."

"Yeah, that would make me angry, too," I say. "Let's get underneath that wall of anger. What age comes to mind when you picture yourself as a very little girl?"

"Hmm.. about seven," she says. "I'm in my room, but putting on this sparkly pink dress. I was definitely more carefree back then, and silly."

"Where did that spark go?" I ask.

"I'm not sure. I know I was a daddy's girl," she says softly. "At least I wanted to be."

"Can you tell us what you mean?" I ask, as I look at the group to see how Charlie and Eddie are doing.

"I tried so hard, I was a good kid. But his love had to be earned," she wipes a tear from her cheek. "I will never leave my little girl the way he left me."

"What did that little seven-year-old girl need?" I guide her.

Eddie hands her the tissue box, and Melissa blows her nose. "She needed to be told she was good enough, that she didn't have to earn his love." Tears are pouring down her face and her expression looks so young, as if she's that seven-year-old little girl sitting right before our very eyes.

I look over at Charlie. "Can you sit over on that side?" I motion to the chair near Melissa.

He gets up and changes seats.

"Charlie, can you say these words: Melissa, you are such a good daughter. You needed me to be there for you."

Charlie repeats the words, "Melissa, you're such a good daughter. I should've been there for you." I can see his eyes are glossy.

"You deserved that. You deserved more than I gave you. You are lovable exactly as you are," I look at Melissa as I continue to guide Charlie in this exercise.

As Charlie repeats the words, tears are rolling down both his cheeks and Melissa's. In this process, he and Eddie are also working through their own abandonment issues. I feel a stinging sensation in my chest. I'm tearing up a bit, too.

"What are you needing in this very moment?" I ask.

"That feels really good to hear. I need time to take this in. Can we stop for now?" Melissa asks.

"Yes we can. Let's take a breath and check in everyone," I say.

"Inhaling relaxation," we pause together, "and exhaling tension." We exhale in unison.

"Thank you everyone for having the courage to be vulnerable and do this healing work today. Each and every one of you now has the job of giving yourself that nurturance and unconditional love you've needed since you were those little kids. You're now in charge of parenting that inner child. And Melissa, remember when you're trying to be so perfect as a wife and a mom. The reality is, being *imperfect* is perfect."

We close the group with self-care intentions and feedback.

*   *   *   *

I see a notification pop up on my phone.

Natalia: Sunkissed at noon?

How does she know my schedule by now? She just pays attention; she cares.

Me: Yes, please :)

There's that familiar rush. A warm sensation runs through my veins, and I can feel the blood pumping through my heart. I can't tell if it starts when I see her name on the screen, or when I imagine her touch, or think of her lips, or if it's the thrill of not knowing what this lunch will be like. Every single moment with her is its own unique adventure. I hold my face as I smile to myself, and tuck my hair behind my ear. I glance at the clock above the couch, and it reads 11:51 a.m. I don't have a noon or one p.m. patient today. Perfect; we have two hours. She's probably already gotten us a table and ordered our drinks. I throw my keys into my wristlet purse, grab my phone and flip the *Jelina King - In Session* sign over to *Jelina King - Out of Office*. I whip around and bump into Mike, who was exiting his office with the standard expression on his face that all of us therapists have when we're trying to maximize the ten minutes between patients and use the restroom, refill our tea, write our patient notes, and hesitate to sacrifice one of those precious minutes for a chat with another human being.

"Woah, buddy!" he says. "So, ya actually leave that cave and eat lunch nowadays?"

He thinks he's so funny. Normally, I'd roll my eyes. I even found myself wincing after about the 27th time he called me Buddy. But not today. Today, I feel a giggle escape me and I think it's sweet that he even notices my self-care.

"I'm going to Sunkissed on Ocean," I reply, somewhat proud that I do things these days like go to Sunkissed on Ocean.

Mike's refilling his mug with hot water, and I swear he's squinting at me. Really. Across his forehead, and his crinkled eyebrows, I can read the words, Who are you?

"Ha! Alrighty, let me know how that goes, will ya?" and he's already bouncing back to his office.

I maneuver around him and am almost out the door when I look down at my heels. No way. "Flip-flops," I say aloud. I turn around and re-enter my office. In the bottom drawer are my California version of what I imagine New Yorkers have for lunchtime walks. I remember putting these flip-flops in here when I first moved into the office, and thought it was a brilliant idea. I also knew deep down that if I was really honest with myself, they would be used a total of zero times, because that would mean getting my body outside of this office to walk down the street to the beach. But instead of that, I opted to stay inside from the time my first patient walked in, eating my pre-packed salads with a plastic fork, and staying straight through until the last patient walked out, only to go straight home.

I slip off my heels, and check the time again: 11:53 a.m. I see the hot pink Havaiana lettering on the blue sandal straps staring at me from my drawer. My favorite part about these is the blue and white vintage palm tree beach print background on them, with the words Sun Sea Salt Surf stamped on them in pink. They're thrilled when I pull them out, letting my heels take their place. Just putting these flip-flops on makes me feel like I'm on vacation. I'm officially not in work mode, and there's a blend of calm and anticipation that washes over me. Much better.

I grab my notebook and stick a pen inside the spiral bound spine, along with my keys and purse. I head out of the office, down the steps and onto the sidewalk outside of my building. The soft slap of my flip-flops relaxes me as I anticipate seeing Natalia again. I feel butterflies for some reason thinking about how this time I'll be visiting her own restaurant *with* her. The salt air smell of the ocean invites me outside, and seagulls caw overhead as I pass the old man with his guitar. He's strumming a Jack Johnson song today. As usual, I wave, but he doesn't look up. You just gotta love this guy. Sometimes I can even hear him during sessions from my office upstairs when I leave the balcony window open. He's my soundtrack to these days.

From the street, I can see a wide view of the ocean. There are tiny sailboats far in the distance near the horizon, and about a dozen surfers are on the water. Most of them are straddling their boards as they sit and wait for a good wave. A few are paddling out fast, and I catch one popping up onto her board and riding a decent-sized swell. Kombis, Bugs and Mini Coopers are parked on the side of the road. My favorite is the convertible Mini with a two-toned teal-and-white paint job.

I wonder if these surfers are out here every day while I'm inside making notes and eating lunch at my desk. I imagine they work for one of the tech companies on Olympic Drive. They have their morning nonfat lattes, start every office meeting with a five-minute meditation, have optional yoga and Tai Chi classes at their disposal, then do their coding and social media development for a few hours, grab a kale wrap from the organic café, and land on the water to take a midday break and hit the surf. Because, why not? And I don't mind.

I stop when I see the familiar green bench. I take a seat and open up my notebook to a blank page, putting pen to paper for the first time in a long while.

June 20, 2023

Growing up, I can still remember sitting on this very bench even as a little girl when Mom would bring us out here for a beach day.

My eyes lift away from my page and catch my own personal movie happening in front of me. I return to my notebook.

The view today happens to be partially blocked by what look like movie set trailers and lighting props. I think that's Kelly Slater wrapping up a surf session. He must be in his early fifties by now, and I'm sure he's still a rock star on the waves. But right now, he's in front of several cameras and a large crowd of onlookers, watching from behind a taped off area. From here, he looks hotter than in photos I've seen on the covers of surfing magazines at the market. Two photographers are running ahead of him, and a drone is hovering overhead catching a wider angle. He's carrying his surfboard in one hand, and a gallon of water in the other. His wetsuit is hanging halfway off of his body at the waist, like a banana peel that's pulled back, showing off his dark bronze skin to all of us passersby on Ocean Avenue. His muscles are glistening from the sun hitting him at the perfect angle, highlighting his shoulders and triceps as he walks along the sand towards the parking lot, where a shiny black E Class Mercedes waits for him. The obvious guess would be that this shoot is for Mercedes, but for all I know, it could be for Chase Bank. When he gets to his sleek ride, the photographers anticipate his moves and prepare to capture the good shots. He lifts the bottle of water over his head, and slowly pours it onto his chestnut hair, drenching his body.

"Wow," I exhale.

"Enjoying the view?" Natalia whispers in my ear, as she slowly wraps her arms around my shoulders and chest from behind.

I jump, clocking her on the chin with my fist and dangerous pen. "Oh my God, I'm so sorry! Hi, yes, um," I say, blushing and with a small laugh in my breath. "I thought we were meeting at Sunkissed."

"We will," she says, standing up and rubbing her chin with *so* much exaggeration, it takes every ounce of willpower for me to not just kiss her right here. "But it'll be even better if we walked there together," she says.

I close up my notebook and put my pen in its place, away from doing any more harm. She takes my hand, and I stand up and melt. I feel ten pounds lighter, and I swear on everything that a breeze of glitter is tickling my entire body—the touch of her fingertips somehow surges all the way to my ears and across my heart, and I can still feel her breath on the back of my neck. Can she tell my body's responding to her right now? Every time we're around each other, it feels like we drift to another time, another dimension. Everything around us is more colorful and sparkling, music is playing around us, life just feels lighter. And I like the feel of her hands against mine, they're soft and smooth. She's just so easy to be around.

"Hold on a sec," I say. We stop for a moment. "Time seems to stand still with us, so if I don't do this, I can bet anything I'll be totally late for my next patient," I say, setting the timer on my phone.

Natalia smiles. "We'll make the most of our minutes together." The look in her eyes makes it a promise.

We make it to Sunkissed Café, and the vibe's different than any other time I've been here. As we walk up the stone steps, the hostess greets us and smiles brightly at Natalia. The hostess is almost unrecognizable wearing a smile rather than the scowl she dons every other time I've been here. The way the staff is treating us, I feel like I'm with a celebrity—or part of her VIP crew at least. The hostess guides us past the tall palm trees lining the walkway, past the millennials on their laptops, and the koi pond where I've sat with Sarah and Helen. Piano and guitar music fills the restaurant and carries us through to the back.

"We're eating in the kitchen?" I ask Natalia.

"Perhaps," she teases.

The hostess turns around a bit, and looks at us both with darting eyes. She feels our chemistry. It's undeniable. "This way," she says. From this angle, I swear I just saw her raise her eyebrows and widen her eyes. Is she jealous?

We reach a spiral staircase, and the hostess bids us farewell. "Enjoy," she says. I could hear the eye-roll in her voice. She's back to her usual self. I'm surprised she was in a pleasant mood. At least she stuck it out for the entire walk.

"Right this way." Natalia gestures to the staircase and I follow where her hand is pointing. I love the look in her eyes; she's looking at me like I'm the only person in the world. She has the ability to make me feel so beautiful and special, the exact opposite of how I've felt all my life. I don't want to disappear, I don't want to be invisible or silent or cower.

"I wonder what you've got up your sleeve, Missy," I say to her, grabbing the handrail and she's following close behind me on this mysterious lunch journey. I'm breathing a bit heavily after the hike up the stairs. "Wow, I need to get in shape!"

"I like your shape." Her fingertips graze my hip. She takes my hand as we climb the last few steps to the top. "This is my own private getaway. But we do rent it out for special business events and weddings sometimes," she says.

After what I think feels like eight flights of stairs, we're on the roof. "Oh my God! This view is incredible," I say. "I've been here so many times with

Sarah and Helen, and we had no idea this café even had a rooftop section."

I take in the breathtaking scene. We have a 180-degree view of the ocean. The breeze kisses my face as my eyes land on the wood-framed sofas and oversized chairs, with their plush cream-colored cushions adorned with colorful pillows. Lush plants, tall and short palm trees, and bright flowers are distributed throughout this large area. White cloth umbrellas offer shade in this hidden sanctuary. A fire pit rests in the center. As I take in the view, I see the flames reach for the sky, and there's a synchronicity between the orange fire, the salty beach air, and the serene ocean.

I walk over to the waist-high glass wall. I can see Surfer's Park from here. The moms and dads I typically envy are out there pushing their kids on swings. I see a couple of moms sitting on a bench with toddlers scooping sand in the sandbox, and I can bet anything they're chatting about which trendy new preschool they're interviewing for. Surfers are floating in the water, and one is paddling out to catch a wave. I look further out and try to see my house. It's not too far from the water, and I should be able to see it from here. My eyes dart back and forth and I'm squinting to try to find it.

"Hey beautiful, lunch is ready." Natalia startles me a bit. She's standing next to me, but she's somehow managed to get close enough behind me that I feel her lips next to my ear. Her words send a tingle from the tip of my ear across my skin and I can feel goosebumps rise on my arm. Her hand rests on the small of my back. "I asked Tom to time it so that we don't waste our precious minutes together. I know you have to get back to your patients, and this isn't our last stop," she says.

We sit down at one of the wooden tables near the fire pit. I can see the waves crashing, and I feel like I'm on top of the world. Tom sets three plates in front of us. The round plate holds a towering burger with a side of glazed carrots. One square plate is piled with edamame sprinkled with sea salt, while another is empty, for the edamame shells.

I place my napkin in my lap. "I take it we're sharing this giant?"

"It's pretty filling, and I thought we might want to save room for dessert later," she says.

"I don't think I'll be hungry for the rest of the week after we down this thing!" I say.

We take turns trying to get our mouths around the burger. It doesn't fit in my mouth and starts to fall apart. I swear they served us a portion big enough to feed three large men. I reach for my fork and knife and Natalia interrupts me by feeding me another bite. Why is everything about her sensual? Even the way she's feeding me this monstrous burger right now. She's successful in her attempt to make it in my mouth and my teeth grab onto a blend of pure heaven. I always take notes on these unforgettable foods, as if I'm ever going to make something like this at home. This one seems easy but I know it would be a flop in my own kitchen: arugula, truffle aioli, marinated tempeh burger, Swiss cheese, and sliced avocado (because it's not a Cali burger without avocado, of course). I guess the complicated part will be making the aioli sauce. Even thinking about getting all the ingredients for just one part of the recipe blocks me from making future home cooking plans for this one.

Tom drops off two water glasses and gives us our privacy. We down the water. Conversation is easy. We flow from where we've travelled to ideas for books we want to write someday. I take the edamame between my teeth, squeezing out the seeds, and tossing the soft shell on the empty plate. I do the same with two more. It has something else on it aside from the sea salt. "Butter?" I ask.

Natalia shakes her head. "A ginger and garlic sauce," she says.

"Delicious." I take another edamame in my mouth and squeeze the seeds out.

We finish about three-quarters of our burger and our water glasses are empty. Natalia checks her phone and says, "It's 12:40. Do you have time for a little walk before you head back to the office?"

"I do. Once he brings us the bill, we can head out," I say.

"It's already taken care of," she says as she stands up and takes my hand.

"Oh! Of course. I feel stupid." How could I say that to the owner of her own restaurant? Ugh. Why don't I have common sense sometimes? I'm such an idiot. She's consistent, attentive and thinking two steps ahead every time. "Why are you so good to me?" I ask. She smiles and takes my hand.

We stroll the SM Beach Boardwalk, continuing our conversation. "When was your first real kiss?" she asks me.

"Real? As in, not a peck on the cheek?" Why am I blushing? I feel like a teenager.

"Real, as in the first kiss that really moved you, and made your entire body tingle," she says. We're holding hands and I'm a little nervous that one of my colleagues will see me with someone who's not my husband. But am I really doing something wrong?

Is it wrong to finally feel good around someone? To have someone appreciate me, to care about my opinions even when they don't match theirs, to take care of me rather than watch me exhaust myself taking care of them? I look around, and feel Natalia's thumb caressing mine. I let myself fall back into a trance.

"I'd kissed my boyfriend of course, but you're asking about a kiss that *moved* me," I breathe in deeply and a smile crosses my face. "So we were both 19. She was someone I just met on a trip," I say. I'm getting butterflies saying this out loud.

"She?" Natalia asks with a smile. We follow the boardwalk, dodging tourists, moms in Lululemon pushing strollers, skateboarders and surfers with their boards in tow.

"Yeah. Oh my gosh, this is so weird," I say, and bite a hangnail off of one of my fingers. "I've never openly talked about this with anyone besides Dylan or my therapist. I would die if my family knew I've been with women."

"Wait, been with? I thought we were talking about first innocent kisses. Ok, I'm all ears," she says.

My heart's racing. "Oh! I didn't sleep with her. I mean, I've slept with women, but not her, and not a lot of women, just—I kissed her, but nothing happened—you know…" Ugh, I'm rambling!

Natalia hushes my jumbled thoughts by paus-
ing our walk in front of a lady selling freshly cut mangos from a cart. She pulls us under the cart's shady
striped umbrella. Mango Lady repeats to the crowd,
"Mangos, six dollars! Mangos, six dollars!" Natalia's
chestnut eyes are inviting me closer. She's doing that
thing again where she's managed to get us completely
alone. The sounds of people walking by and cars on
the road fade into the background. She hands the
woman a ten-dollar bill and waves for her to keep the
change. Mango Lady smiles and hands N a t a l i a a
clear plastic cup overflowing with ripe sliced mango.
We each grab a slice and resume our walk. She holds
the cup between us every so often so I can reach for
another slice.

I explain, "It was up in Santa Cruz. You know
where that is?" Why am I stalling? This is such a juve-
nile topic, easy and light. She knows I'm stalling, but
she goes with it.

"I've never been, but it's that beachy San Fran
area with a bunch of stoners, right?" she asks.

"I guess you could say that. But isn't anywhere you go in California full of stoners nowadays?"

"Good point," she replies.

"It's about an hour outside of San Francisco,"
I continue. "It's such a cool area. I drove up there with

a guy I was dating at the time. My mom hated him, and I don't blame her. I have no idea what I was doing with him. He didn't have a car, was rude to me, he used my truck to go to band practice, and I found out he was also skipping band practice to hook up with one of our friends."

Natalia doesn't give her opinion just yet, and lets me go on another tangent. She has so much patience for my rambling.

"So anyway, he and I were over there visiting some of his friends who went to UCSC. Oh my God, that campus is just absolutely gorgeous! We have to go some time." Did I just say that?

"I'd like that," Natalia responds casually.

I smile uncomfortably and play with my hair. "Does everyone go on tangents like this?"

"You'd know that more than I would, doctor," she says.

"I'm not a—"

"…doctor. I know, I know. But to me, therapist, psychologist, doctor, you're all the same," she says.

I have to rein in the nerd in me and stop myself from explaining the difference and just focus.

"Ok, so you were in Santa Cruz and a hot blonde came out of nowhere and gave you the kiss of a lifetime?" she asks.

"Wow, you're good. Pretty much," I say. "My boyfriend and I were walking around with his friends all over that amazing campus. I swear it's in the middle of the forest. These college kids get to walk down pathways and across wooden bridges to their classes, under hundreds of giant redwood trees." I close my eyes. "I can smell that air right now. It's like fruits and berries and pine and fresh air, and just raw nature. Their dorms are tucked right in there, in the middle of this majestic forest."

"It sounds amazing," Natalia says.

"It really is. And we walked around the little town in the afternoon. It's so cute over there. Kinda reminds me of Big Bear, ya know?" I say. "But I used to get so socially awkward, and I didn't know these people. They were his friends, so I was really insecure and never comfortable, and just wanted us to keep doing things and not just sit around and talk, because that's just the worst. I've always just hated small talk, never knowing what to say, probably because I honestly didn't care about what they were talking about. I either wanted to disappear during slow moments or when everyone's just hanging around and talking, or I was desperate for us to keep doing things and stay busy and active. I'm good with that. Anyway, at night we hung out at a bonfire on the beach."

"So here's where the magic happens," Natalia says.

"Yes! Oh my God, and it was so sweet." I can hear myself speaking louder and in a higher register. All the memories are flooding back as if I'm right there at 19 again. "So we're all sitting around at this bonfire. And I just loved every second of it because being at the beach is my favorite thing in the world! There were about five of us and then some other people joined later. I don't know where they came from. A couple of guys were playing guitar, and my boyfriend was helping keep the fire going and getting more wood from the truck. He was so wasted, and telling loud stories and everyone was laughing. I seem to always date the life of the party and I'm the wallflower."

"But someone ended up seeing this beautiful wallflower." Natalia helps me get to the point.

"We were all just kicking back and listening to the music and sitting around a bonfire. It was such a gorgeous night. And then this girl came over to me," I say. "I hadn't seen her the whole day, so she must've been one of those randoms who ended up joining us later. She sat next to me on one of the blankets we'd spread out, and started talking to me about one of the guys who was playing guitar. I don't remember what she was saying, but I do remember being entranced by her lips. And every once in a while, she'd touch my hand when she was trying to make a point." I slow to a stop, and Natalia follows suit. I look into her eyes and take a deep breath.

"You know those moments when you go through something so intense at the time, and then years and years later, you can still feel it on your skin?" I look at Natalia without waiting for her to an-swer. I graze my fingers along the top of her hand and across her arm. I can't believe I'm touching her like this. And she's letting me. Not criticizing, not sham-ing me, not pinching me. Just respectful and sweet. "Like this, you know?" I whisper.

"This is one of those skin moments I hope we always remember," she responds, placing her hand on top of mine.

"I like these skin moments with you," I say.

"Can you tell me more about your first skin moment with Miss Blondie?" Natalia asks. We've fall-en into this pattern now a few times where I get dis-tracted and she finds a way to pull me back in.

"Do I sense some jealousy?" I tease.

"Do you still talk to her?" Natalia answers with a question, and for a second I can't tell if she's joking or not. Is she jealous? If she is, I kind of like it. She actually cares.

"Oh my gosh, you're so cute! You're a little jealous of Miss Blondie. Well, rest assured, we only sext when I'm bored," I say as I kiss her hand.

"Very funny." She playfully punches my arm, puts her arm around my shoulder and guides us into motion. We're walking away from the pier and I can see the roller coaster and ferris wheel at the end of the pier.

"So we were sitting by that bonfire with everyone, and she asks me to go with her by this cove area because she had to pee," I say. "And I swear my boyfriend couldn't care less. I don't even think he remembered I was there, to tell you the truth. And this girl and I end up walking quite a ways. I remember it was really dark, but we ended up getting to this hidden cove where it was like the quietest spot at the beach. She goes into the cove area and pees. It takes her for what feels like forever. So I walked over to the shore and waited for her by the water. I kept dipping my toes in and out of the water, and it was super cold. I remember I was shivering a little and of course my hoodie was in my truck. And I could see the moonlight hit the water in such a way that it looked like a painting." I move my hand as if I'm holding a paintbrush, painting the scene for us.

"She comes back out of the cove and takes my hand. I'd never even held a girl's hand before. I mean, maybe my friends? But I don't know. I really don't remember a girl ever holding my hand the way she did. You know? And my heart was beating so fast, and my palms were so sweaty. I remember being so embarrassed that I tried to pull my hand away to wipe it on my jeans. But then she took both of my hands and clasped them in hers so that we were facing each other under that moonlight, and time slowed down. She said, 'Close your eyes.' And I did. I can still feel that nervous excitement in my veins like I did that night. I felt so ugly at that time in my life and was wondering why she was even giving me the time of day. I mean, there I was, standing with this cute blonde girl, and I was the person who hated how I looked so much that I always wished I could be invisible. I literally cut out every single one of my pictures in all my yearbooks. But I was standing there about to have my first real kiss. Then, all of a sudden, I felt her hands unclasp, but she didn't let go of me."

I close my eyes and run my hands alongside my arm as if I've been transported under that same

Santa Cruz moonlight. "She slid both of her hands along my arms, up to my shoulders and my neck and then held my face." I cradle my chin and cheekbones in my hands. "And for the first time in my life, I felt the softest pillow lips press against mine. And her tongue barely touched mine and it was like our mouths were making love." I feel like I'm in a dream as I keep my eyes closed, telling my story and reliving that magical night under the moonlight. "It was the most—" Just like how a dream can turn into reality, I'm both startled and entranced when I feel Natalia's lips touch mine. I'm breathing her in as I keep my eyes closed as my brain blends the 19-year-old blonde and Natalia's kiss into one moment. I taste the sweet mango, and feel her gentle mouth playing with mine.

I almost lose my balance. We unlock lips and open our eyes. "I never knew the memory of my first real kiss could become even more special," I say, catching my breath.

"You deserve to feel special everyday," Natalia says.

"I have an idea," I say, as I take her hand, leading us towards the pier. "We still have some time before I need to be back for my next patient."

We walk underneath the words Santa Monica Coaster written in sea-green letters on a wooden sign.

"Are you serious? We're gonna go on that thing right now?" She says.

I don't know what's gotten into me, but right now I'm loving this carefree feeling. "It'll be fun. Why not," I say more as a command rather than a question. I pull her towards the line.

Her head tilts back as she looks up at the monstrous roller coaster. Its track circles all around the pier.

The ferris wheel is right next to it, stopping and going as passengers get on and off. I can smell churros from a stand next to it, and hear the symphony of rides, carnival games and people cheering and screaming. A loud roar charges overhead as the coaster runs on the track and barrels past us. I've seen it a thousand times when I head to the office every morning, and it's on all the postcards and tourist paraphernalia in the markets in town.

"Another first together," I say to Natalia as we reach the back of the line. We're packed like sardines between the narrow railings that go from the wooden planks of the pier, and take us up along a staircase I'd guess is a couple stories high. I'm wondering if there's one other person in line who's on their lunch break from work and just happened to want to take a ride on a roller coaster. You never know.

We inch our way up the staircase, shoulder to shoulder. I can feel Natalia's tension, and she hasn't said a word since we first got into this line. "You ok?" I ask.

"Eh, kinda. I dunno. Not really," she says. She's gripping the rail so tightly, I can see her knuckles are white.

"When was the last time you were on one of these?" I ask. It's a new feeling to see her vulnerable for the first time. I'm more attracted to her in this moment than ever before.

"I dunno. But the last time, I had a panic attack. And I think the time before that, too. Or maybe it was after I got off the ride. I dunno. I just remember saying I'd never get on one again," she says.

"Oh my gosh, I had no idea! We don't have to ride. It's not a big deal. We can back out of line and go play some of those games over there," I say and point to a blue awning about 50 yards away. "I just thought it would be fun," I say.

Natalia looks like she's seen a ghost. I have no annoyance towards her. She could change her mind a dozen times and I wouldn't be bothered. But I say one stupid thing, and I can't stop beating myself up.

"Hey, I'm right here with you, ok?" I say.

"I have to do this. I can't back out. I want to do this. I'm just so embarrassed right now. You seeing me like this. I'm freaking out. But I have to do this," she's stammering. Her speech is rapid. Her nervousness is endearing.

"I'm right here," I say again. All I've ever been certain of in my life is that my superpower is connection. I'm not the one who loves crowds, or the one with the entertaining stories, or the most brilliant in a room. But I can connect when someone's down or needs love and attention. I can take someone from panic to calm. From freaking out to ok. "Where did you say you grew up again?" I ask her as a way to distract her.

"What?" She asks, without moving her eyes from the coaster.

I hold her hand and we take three steps up the staircase. We're almost at the platform where the line splits, and everyone stands where they'll be on the roller coaster. There are two people ahead of us. They're probably a couple, so I'm guessing we have about 60 more breaths until we're next to climb into the coaster. Her hand is shaking and sweaty.

"Can you tell me where you grew up?" I try again. She's not even looking at me, just fixated on the rollercoaster as it roars along the track. We hear the cheers and loud screams and laughter.

"Uh…Florence," she says, still not even turning towards me, holding onto the railing and my hand for dear life.

"Florence, Italy. It's breathtaking there. And when did you move to the States?"

I can see her balancing freaking out and trying not to be rude to me. "Um, six." The couple ahead of us moves up onto the platform and walks to where they'll end up in the back of the coaster. The roller coaster hasn't made it back around the pier yet, and I can hear it in the distance. Her eyes are fixated on exactly where the coaster is on the track.

"Six, wow! I can't imagine moving countries at six years old. Where did you guys move to when you first came out here?" I continue. Her hands are slippery from all the sweat, but I hold on.

"Santa Clarita," She pushes the words out as if they may be the last she utters before this roller coaster ride leads to her doom.

"You're kidding! I was born in Valencia. What part of Santa Clarita were you guys in?"

"The South side," she says. Her eyes follow the coaster as it gets louder and closer, rounding the corner. It screeches to a halt, and the passengers unbuckle their seatbelts, lift the safety bar, and climb out onto the opposite side of the platform. I can hear teenagers cheering and one woman laughing loudly, telling her friends she can't believe how crazy that last drop was! Great, thanks lady.

"Oh my God. I think I'm going to puke." With that, Natalia confirms to me that she definitely heard that laughing lady too, who probably raised her freak-out level a couple notches. I see an open spot all the way at the front of the coaster conveniently waiting for us. The attendant yells, "C'mon, you're up! Step in and buckle up!"

I can hear Natalia's heartbeat from where I'm standing. We climb into the coaster, fumble with the clunky seat belts and pull the safety bar down. She's so vulnerable and looks so innocent. She's an entirely differently person right now. This side of her is so endearing. Her eyes are locked straight ahead. People are still climbing in, and the anticipation is pretty crazy. I'm waiting for Natalia to shout that she can't do it. But everyone's locked and loaded, and it's now or never. Here we are, riding through fear together.

"Did you ever go to that Tommy's Burger on The Old Road and...what was the name of that other street?" I ask, hoping my deflection strategy will start calming her nerves.

"Huh? Tommy's Burger?" She looks at me for a whole five seconds. "I used to work there. That was my very first job."

"Really? My elementary school was right across the street! We used to walk over there on Fridays. I remember they put this ketchup sauce or something all over the food, right?"

"Chili," she says. Her eyes are now fixed on the attendant, who holds our lives in her hands. She splashes more anxiety onto the scene when she interrupts my deflection strategy with the intercom.

"Keep your hands and arms inside at all times! Enjoy the ride." Is it really necessary for you to yell into the intercom, lady?

"Chilly?" I ask.

"What? Oh, chili. Tommy's puts chili all over everything."

I can smell the chili in my mind as I remember those greasy burgers.

The roller coaster pushes forward, crawling for a moment, then getting a bit bumpy as it increases its speed.

"Oh God... oh God," Natalia's whispering, but I can hear her clearly over the rumble of the coaster.

"What job did you have after Tommy's?" I ask, as we bump along the track. I need to get on this, or she's going to have a panic attack.

"I—I was a cashier at Longs Drugstore." She forces the words out. The coaster is getting louder.

"Cool. For how long!" I shout.

"About a year," she says, gripping the safety bar. Her white knuckles reveal her anxiety level is still high.

"Ok, and then after Longs Drugstore?" I ask.

Natalia ignores my question, or doesn't hear it. I can't tell. We're carried above the crowds of tourists and are now facing the ocean. You'd think we were on a helicopter overlooking the water. "The ocean," she breathes out. I look out where I think her eyes are focused.

Whoever engineered this coaster must have carefully situated it to have this exact view in order to prevent panic attacks. The loud clicking sounds and slight jolts come at a steady pace as the coaster climbs the incline. My heart rate is increasing a little, and it's a familiar excitement I remember from when I would come here as a little girl. The ocean view is breathtaking. It looks like diamonds are floating on the water. An image of my inner child from my dream flashes before my eyes. She's writing in her notebook, just as she was when I saw her on my kitchen floor, but in my mind's eye she's panicked and the look on her face is so fearful it stings my heart. I want to hold onto that image for just a little longer and I'm drawn to her and want to learn more about her, but I blink her away.

The coaster reaches its peak, then slows down to an eerie pace. We all know what's coming next. "I can't do this! I can't do this!" Natalia shouts. The coaster drops about 50 feet. "Oh my God!" She screams so loudly, I'm certain the entire Santa Monica Pier stopped in their tracks.

The coaster rounds the bend at a speed even I wasn't prepared for. I'd guess we're doing about 60 miles per hour, but I have no idea, we could be going 20. The pressure presses us back into the seat. It's not giving us a break just yet. Isn't this supposed to be a family park?

"What job did you have after Longs?" I try again, as the coaster finally eases up and calms to a low growl. I don't think I've ever asked for someone's entire resume as an anxiety reduction technique before. But this is all I can come up with right now.

"In a law office, then a pharmacy," Natalia answers. Her breath syncs with mine and I'm guiding her in relaxation exercises without her even realizing it. I think I might see an actual smile on her face. I know her anxiety is still through the roof, though, because we haven't locked eyes for even a second since we got on this thing.

I put my hand on hers, and she loosens her grip on the safety bar. The ride is on its final roll and now just coasting. "Wow, I should've asked where haven't you worked. Anywhere else?" I ask.

"A Pre-School. Two years," she says. The coaster comes to a complete stop. I can feel her relief.

"Aww, that's adorable!" I say. We climb out, step onto the platform and walk down the stairs. "And now you're a hot, successful entrepreneur."

I take her by the hand, we make it out of the coaster area and I stop us in the middle of the crowded pier. We're right back where we started, standing underneath the words *Santa Monica Coaster*. Kids and teenagers are dodging us to have their turn on the ride, lovebirds release their clasped hands to get around us, seagulls sing to us from overhead, and the scent of warm churros mixed with the salty ocean breeze fill the air. "Congratulations," I say, and lean in close enough to kiss her. Our mouths are less than an inch apart, and I can feel her breath against my lip. "You just made it through an entire ride without a panic attack. I'm proud of you."

Natalia makes eye contact with me for the first time since before we got in line. "I guess this was my turn to be vulnerable."

We stay in this connected space for several more breaths. I lean in, craving her. I need her, I want her, right here and now in this moment. The sounds and colors and life around us fade away. I'm pulled towards her. Her arms wrap around me; the same way they did the night of our sound bath. My entire body is in ecstasy when her soft lips touch mine. We're slowly letting our mouths explore one another. Between tender kisses, our tongues lightly play. Her hips are beckoning me to reciprocate. My fingers find their way to the belt loops on her jeans, responding to her that I'll stay for a little longer. I come up for air and put my finger to my mouth, feeling the outline of my lips, as if to secure the memory of this very moment, of how it's possible for two people to be gentle and attentive to one another.

My phone alarm chimes, an intrusive reminder that we must transport back into the real world. I snooze it, close my eyes and let my lips touch hers, and our tongues taste and play gently for a moment longer. I don't want this to moment to end.

It chimes again, attempting to pull us away from our ecstasy. Maybe this is a sign that I need to have morals. I'm a married woman for God's sake. I scroll through my texts. Client, client, Helen — my dad.

Dad: Please call me

My body tenses up.

"What's going on?" Natalia nudges at me.

"It's my dad," I say. It's taking me a moment to digest what I'm feeling. My typical panic mixed with annoyance is gone. Really, it is. I don't feel that stinging in my chest, and my palms are dry.

My thumb scrolls up to his number and hovers over it for a bit. Ok, hello panic. There you are. My heart is pounding fast.

I look up at Natalia. "Am I really doing this? What happens next, then? I don't even know if I want a relationship. Does this mean I approve of him not protecting me and defending his brother molesting me?"

"He's a human being who didn't know any better and tried his best as a dad," Natalia says.

I press the number and hear it ringing. My thumb floats over the *End* button for three rings. I press *End* and toss the phone in my bag. My heart is racing. I can't do it.

"Try it. See what it's like to say it," she says.

"Ugg, I can't."

"I forgive you," she helps me.

I stare at her.

"I forgive you," she says again. "Forgiving someone else is not really about the other person, you know. It's about releasing yourself from holding onto resentments and letting that person rent space in your head. The longer you hold onto this, the longer it will keep affecting how you let people treat you and how you love. You've been accepting the love you think you deserve."

"I forgive you," I say aloud, as I reorient myself back to reality: standing here by the ocean, next to a person who truly cares about what's going on with me and what will make me happy.

I look down at my phone again.

Dad: Please call me

I scroll down to his number.

It's ringing…and ringing… now silence. I can feel him on the other end of the line. Natalia holds my hand.

"Jelina? Is this you?"

My mouth is partly open, but no words are coming out. I pull the phone away from my face. It's so strange to hear his voice. It's softer than I remember.

"Jelina?" I bring the phone back to my ear.

"Hi," I say.

"Jelina, oh my God! It's you," he says, just as shocked as I am.

"I'm sorry it took me this long to call you."

Natalia rubs my thumb with hers, as our hands stay clasped.

"I'm sorry. I'm sorry for... everything." His voice is shaky. I can almost see his tears in my mind.

"Dad, I don't want you to worry about me anymore. Please know I'm ok," I say as a tear falls onto my cheek. I'm

He's silent, but I can hear him sniffling.

"We're ok," I say. "You and me. I'm not holding onto anything any longer."

"Oh dear, I love you," he says through tears, and breathing heavily.

"Take care, Dad. I have to go, please take care of yourself."

I press *End* on the phone.

Natalia grazes her hand across my cheek, wiping my tears away. "You ok?"

I close my eyes and breathe in the ocean air. A wave of calm washes over me. My shoulders feel lighter. "Yeah, I think so. I couldn't stay on the phone any longer. I just couldn't."

"It's ok," Natalia says.

"This is all so surreal. This day is surreal. Life truly is a dream, isn't it?" I look up at her.

"It really is," she says.

"Maybe this will all sink in at some point," I look out at the ocean.

"All you have to do is put one foot in front of the other. Just keep going," she says, connecting the dots of the freckles on my arm.

"Keep going?"

"Yes, sometimes life nails us, or we want to give up. Or things feel too difficult. Just keep going," she kisses my thumb.

"Thank you for the best lunch break in the history of lunch breaks," I say.

"My pleasure," she kisses my lips one last time and just when I come to and open my eyes again, she's gone.

I breathe in my Natalia drug as I float in bliss walking along Ocean Avenue on my way back to the office.

Strange, guitar guy isn't out here in his usual spot. I gasp and put my hand to my heart as it hits me. "Dad?!" I say to myself.

Chapter Thirteen:

The Jump

I pull into the driveway, shut off the engine and see Lily asleep in the backseat next to the groceries I got from the store. I sit in the car for several minutes. *Don't neglect your happiness for anyone. You can live happier beyond your wildest dreams.* Those words won't escape my mind. I'm done living like this; dying like this. It's over. He's never going to change. And Lily deserves a mom who shows her how important it is to take care of herself, and to live in a home where she isn't soaking up all of our tension, but where she can feel safe and carefree. I never want her to feel trapped. We always have a choice, and there's never the right moment to make changes. I get my phone and scroll to Natalia's name.

Me: To say thank you for today would be an understatement. You are magic

Natalia: It's you who is magic

Me: Sleep well xo

Natalia: xo

I take a deep breath. Dylan will be wide awake from now until three in the morning. Add that to the list of arguments and marital distance that started the first year of our marriage. I spent countless nights begging him to come to bed with me, or to lay down with me, longing for him to pleasure me the way he did the very first time. He was the only person to make me climax that way. But those days are over. We've transformed from passionate lovers to distant bitter roommates. He became comfortable refusing to come to bed with me, saying he wasn't tired or not in the mood, and I eventually stopped asking, and surrendered to falling asleep feeling rejected and taken for granted—for years, in every way.

Enough!

I tap Lily's knee and she wakes up. I grab my work bag and groceries, and Lily and I climb out of the car and into the house. Dylan is seated at the dining room table in front of his laptop. I've never known what he does on there. He used to get annoyed and defensive when I would ask. So I stopped asking. I stopped trying anymore. Is he looking at porn? Maybe; it would explain why he isn't as starved for sex as I am. Is he chatting with other women? I don't think so. I do trust him when it comes to monogamy. Did he just add another grand to our debt for something he just had to buy? Probably. It's quiet, I'm clear-headed and calm. Sadly, I think I've officially stopped caring anymore.

"Hey," I say as I set my bag down and walk over to the dining table where he's sitting. Lily's energy perks up a bit and she goes straight to Dylan and sits on his lap.

"Hey, guys." He kisses Lily on the head, looks up at me and leans over as we exchange our obligatory peck on the lips. "How was work?" He asks me with his eyes on the laptop screen and tapping on the keyboard with one hand.

"It was fine," I say, not surprised that I'm at the bottom of his priority list - or even on it? "I'm going to help Lily with her bath and after I put her to bed I really need to talk to you tonight."

"About what?" He looks at me. I usually fall asleep reading to Lily at bedtime.

"Let's talk after she's in bed," I take Lily's hand. C'mon Lily, it's time for your bath, and then we'll read Ellie's Story." She loves her new chapter books, and they make all the difference in getting her into bed.

*   *   *   *

I come back to the dining room and see Dylan's already put the groceries away. Wow.

"Thank you for doing that," I tell him. I sit down at the table across from him. I know I'm catching him off guard, as I never stop and sit this late, or stop and sit—period. I'm always throwing in another load of laundry, doing dishes, or catching up on paperwork.

He can feel I'm different. I have his undivided attention for the first time in seven years.

He closes his laptop. "What's going on?" he asks. He looks genuinely concerned, as if he's seeing me for the very first time in years. We're having uninterrupted eye contact. I haven't seen him look at me, or really see me. I follow his eyes as they examine my face, my arms, and my collarbone. For the first time, I don't feel invisible.

"You've gotten thinner," he says, looking at me from head to toe.

I'm not even going there. "I need to tell you something," I say. I can't believe how calm I am. I'm not crying, I'm not yelling, I'm crystal clear.

"What? What is it?" he asks. He's leaning forward, and his expression is one I can't really decipher.

"I can't do this anymore."

"What are you talking about? What does that even mean?" Alright, I know what his expression is now. Fear. I haven't seen it on him before. "Can't do what?"

"This is so hard for me to say to you. And I don't want to cause you unnecessary pain. I kept thinking all night, 'Who am I to you anymore? Why should I tell you this if it might hurt you?' We don't even act like husband and wife anymore, we're bitter roommates. And I feel so much contempt. I've reached the point of no return. But I don't want to lie to you and say I'm hanging out with a friend or you don't hear from me for hours and I say I was busy. I just don't know how to do this except what I'm doing now, which is to talk about it."

"Just spit it out!" He says. *"What the hell is going on?"*

"I've fallen in love with someone," I say. I'm still surprised by my own calmness. "We were intimate," I confess. I don't know how much to tell him. I just know that my days of being too nice are a thing of the past.

"You were intimate? What the hell does that even mean?" Ok, I know that look on his face quite well. It's the one I hate the most. The one where he thinks I'm the biggest idiot in the room. That motivates me to cut to the chase.

"Exactly. You and I don't even speak the same language." I look down at the table, feeling the shame sting at me a bit. "I want a divorce, Dylan." There they are, the words that for years I never thought would even enter my mind, let alone come out of my mouth. But in this moment, I'm jumping off of the burning sinking ship that's become our marriage.

"What?!" He's looking at me like he's been completely blindsided, but I have no idea how that's possible with the way things have been.

"I've fought, yelled, cried, told you what I want and need, and nothing changes. You know how unhappy I am. But you haven't cared or listened until right this second. Look at me!" I raise my hands in the air, for him to see that I'm skin and bones.

"What do you mean you want a divorce? You've never even brought this up to me before." He's in shock. He's finally stepping out of his own world for a minute, and for the first time is taking in what's happened to our marriage.

"I've never said divorce, you're right. But I've told you how unhappy and stressed I've been for years, and that I didn't sign up to be the breadwinner of the family, or to take care of everything on my own. You've completely taken me for granted! You never come to bed with me, you reject me over and over again. We don't have sex!" Dylan's eyes are glossy now, and I think he and I are both surprised that I'm not rubbing his back and soothing him. "I'm sorry, I just can't run myself into the ground anymore. This is not healthy for us. I'm not going to end up in a hospital with a nervous breakdown."

"I'm so sad that it's gotten to this point. I know it's not fair to you that I stuck it out so long and was unfailingly pleasant and agreeable and just said gave in after so much fighting and caved and did everything for us. You needed to hear No over and over again. No, we can't put that trip to the Caribbean or Sydney on my credit cards and max them out. We need to buy those tickets when we have liquid money, or at least pay our electric bill first. No, we can't drain the 20k of savings I was proud to have earned over the years before I met you. No, you can't quit that job because you don't like that your boss is telling you that you have to be at work on time, or quit the next one because you just don't like being a lawyer anymore, or keeping the surf shop open, or doing personal training, or anything where you have to start from the bottom and be uncomfortable like the rest of us… while I have to stay at mine no matter what because the bills have to be paid somehow."

I don't have any tears right now. They must have dried out from all the years of crying up until this point.

I can't tell if he's more upset that he's losing me, or that he has to figure out what he's going to do for a steady income now. He's crying, but I'm past my breaking point. It's too late.

"Why didn't you tell me that you would divorce me? " Dylan asks.

"You're kidding me," I say. "I shouldn't have to threaten to leave you in order for you to come to bed with your own wife, or for you to be willing to stay in a job so that we're both sharing the weight of the bills together. I never even considered divorce until now. I deserve to be with a partner who notices me, who sees me, who genuinely cares about someone other than himself, who wants to take care of himself, who's willing to get uncomfortable for the sake of us being a team, who both gives and takes equally, and doesn't just take take take to only keep wanting more."

"But I do care," he says. Dylan is wiping tears from his face and has his face in his hands.

"I'm disappearing," I say, tugging on my top. "People at work think I'm anorexic. I've told you this. I'm having panic attacks, I even had one in front of my patient!"

"What about Lily?" He looks me dead in the eyes. "Do you even care about what this will do to her?"

"Lily's not ok *now*! She's four and *still* wetting the bed, she doesn't talk to anyone. She can't make friends at school. She's very unhappy. She feels all of our tension. She needs for us to be healthy and she deserves that. And we're not. Not like this. You know all this, and none of that was enough for you to change? What you needed to hear was a threat that I would divorce you? I refuse to live like this anymore - for her, for me. You know how unhappy I've been, or have you not noticed or even cared? I've tried to say it nicely for years, and cried it, yelled it. Nothing works with you. I never wanted to leave you. Divorce never even crossed my mind all these years. I loved you. I still do." I feel myself softening a bit.

"I love you, too. I want to make this work. Please, baby," he takes my hand. "Don't pull away."

I let his hand rest on mine, and wipe a tear from his cheek with my other hand. "I'm sorry," I say. "We were great early on, hun. It was like a fairytale love story. We clicked in school immediately. I thought you were handsome and funny and charming and we laughed and learned a lot from each other. Our date at atat our favorite restaurant and that incredible night where you pleasured me in a way I never had been pleasured before. You surprised me with picnics and coming home to dinners you'd make and music and candles and bathtubs filled with rose petals. That feels like a whole other lifetime. That's why I stayed for this long, because that's who I married and who I've been hoping would show up again. Now I don't know what to believe. I feel like it was all just good marketing skills to get me in—I signed the dotted line, and had no idea I was signing up for everything to be different after that."

Dylan's eyebrows are furrowed and doing that thing I found cute at one point, but now it just gets under my skin.

He cries hard and pulls his hand away. He's bawling like I've never seen before. I rub his back without even thinking about it. He looks at me, confused. "I can't believe you're so calm," he says. "I can't believe you're quitting - just like that."

"It's not 'Just like that.' I've been killing my-self trying to fight for us to stay together and make this work.

"Who are you in love with?" He asks.

"Her name is Natalia," I can't help but feel my face soften. I try to control it, but I can't. I can see his whole body bulk up. His blood is boiling. And his pain has turned into anger that's building and building.

"*Natalia?!*" He sounds grossed out. "*You're breaking up our family for a dyke?*" My stomach turns with his words. "You're a joke."

I turn around and look down the hall at Lily's bedroom door. "Please keep it down. I don't want to wake her up. I'm sorry. I didn't do this on purpose." I'm still shocked I'm not crying. I'm immediately regretful I've even told him about Natalia because now I look like the reason for the downfall of our marriage. I guess both of us are at fault.

"You want to break up my family over this? I'm going to make your life a living hell. I promise you that," he says. I feel horrible that I've turned him into this angry monster right now, but my mouth won't take back my words. He continues, "Does your mom know you're a dyke?" he spits out, as he gets up and snatches my phone out of my bag.

"What are you doing?!" I grab his arm in an attempt to get my phone from him. I'm panicked he's going to see all the messages between Natalia and me. But he's not doing that. I see him scrolling to my mom's name. He starts texting from my phone and reading out loud as he's typing.

Me: I'm breaking up my family because I'm a selfish dyke

He hits *Send*!?

"*Oh my God! What are you doing??! I can't believe you!*" I yell. I'm pulling on his shirt and arms, trying to get my phone. "*That's my mom!*"

"Watch me. You broke up my family. I'll break up yours."

He's scrolling through my contacts and hitting *Block* and *Delete* on Jake and Jane, his parents, his sister.

I'm in utter shame. I grab his other arm and then get a hold of my phone and pull it from his hand. He shoves me off of him and I fall to the ground. I can't believe this is happening!

I'm frozen on the ground for at least several seconds trying to compute this whole thing. I get back onto my feet and pull at his shirt, tearing it at the neckline. That pisses him off even more and he slaps me across the cheek. "You're a fake ass cunt, and I'll make sure Lily will know the real reason she's from a broken home. That *you* broke up her family."

With that, I give up. I'm defeated. My cheek stings, but I deserve it. Tears are rolling down my face. Apparently tears don't run out.

I never wanted to be a victim and sadly I put myself in that position. He's right. I've been fake. I've been lying my whole life. Maybe I am a lesbian? I don't even know. Or maybe I just don't even know who I am or how to love. I wasn't emotionally equipped to get married. *"I hate you!"* I yell at the top of my lungs.

My heart stops when I see Lily standing in her doorway. I can't even breathe. I'm mortified. What have I done?

Chapter Fourteen:

Shook (June 21, 2023)

I wake up and I'm a bit disoriented, remembering I fell asleep on the sofa. The clock on the oven is pretty far from here, but I think it reads 2:27. I get up and pour myself a glass of water, and put some ice in a bag to press against my cheek. I stand with my back against the kitchen counter, nursing my sore cheek.

As I'm drying my hands, and walking back to the sofa, I remember my new reality. I think Dylan and I are breaking up. I can't believe things got physical tonight. *Us. Dylan and me.* This isn't even who we are. So unreal. I think of Lily's little face in the doorway. I'm so ashamed. We're *that* out of control and this is Lily's world now. We've failed as parents. This isn't why we brought her into the world.

Footsteps creek on the hardwood floor down the hall. Dylan and I meet on the sofa.

"Hey," he says. His eyes are puffy.

"Hey, I'm so lost right now," I say. "I don't even know what to feel or say."

"Babe, I'm sorry about this," he takes over holding the ice pack for me. "I don't know how this even happened. I freaked out."

"It's fine. I deserve it. I'm sorry about everything," I say.

"I don't want to get a divorce," he says, as he looks into my eyes.

"Dylan, we both know we can't keep doing this," I say, and now the tears are falling.

"Baby, I just don't want to lose you," he wipes my tears from my cheek. "It was just a hook up with a woman. We can get through this together," he says and holds my hand. "I believe in us. I'm sorry for what I said last night. And about your mom. I think I had a couple drinks and this is all just so scary if I were to lose you."

I take his hand. "I know you hate when I mention this," I say, "but I really do think you need to talk to someone about your drinking," I say.

"I will. I will do that. You're right," he says. "I can talk to *you*. You help people with this, right?"

"It doesn't work like that," I say.

I look at him with soft eyes. "I'm sorry, but it's over honey. I don't regret anything, even after all this," I say. "But things have changed. We've both changed. We were so in love, and all that's gone. I just can't do this anymore. It's killing all of us. Lily's not ok, I'm not ok, and you're not either."

"You're really giving up on us? You're not even willing to try? I just can't believe you're walking away so easily," he says, rubbing my thumb with his.

"I've been trying, for so long. I just never said the word divorce. I never even considered it. It didn't cross my mind as an option. But I'm exhausted from trying and this isn't healthy for any of us, and I can't try and hope anymore for something that will never change. We're the worst versions of ourselves. And you are a good dad. This doesn't change that. And no matter what happens with us, I don't doubt for a second that we'll continue to raise her together with love," I say, as he pulls his hand away.

Dylan looks as exhausted as I feel. "I don't want to end this." He's staring down at the table, and then up at me with such sad eyes.

I put my hand on top of his. "It feels right, and I really believe it's what we all need." I say, and I'm emotionally exhausted. "Let's sleep. We can figure everything out later. This has been a long night."

He goes back to the bedroom and I return to the sofa. My body feels strangely calm right now.

*   *   *   *

I wake up to a powerful jolt and the eerie sounds of the structure of the house moving. The sofa is jerking back and forth. Having grown up in Southern California, it doesn't startle me. These tremors only last a few seconds. I stay still for a while, my body stiff, since nothing's fallen from the bookshelf. Dylan's snoring down the hall in the bed room.

"Dylan!" I shout. "Dylan, wake up!"

Nothing.

I don't know why I bother. Of course he won't wake up. Let him sleep. There's nothing that could drop onto him over there.

Although we get earthquakes every few years, we're raised to keep the idea in the backs of our minds that we should be prepared for the inevitable Big One. For that reason, our mirror hangs on the other side of the living room, and our bookshelf is securely attached to the wall, positioned so that if it falls, it won't reach the sofa. The house is starting to jolt harder now, and I stand up, losing my balance as the ground moves beneath me. This is not a typical quake.

"Mommy!" Lily cries from her room.

"I'm coming, honey! Stay calm and go under your desk!" Now, the adrenaline is moving through me, charging my body up into high alert and draining away all my sleepiness. I flip the light switch. Nothing happens. Great. I see my phone on the coffee table and turn on the flashlight app so I can find my slippers next to the sofa. I put them on and try to point my phone towards the ground a few feet ahead of me. Lily and I have practiced what to do during an earthquake once a long time ago. I wish we had practiced more often. But they do earthquake drills at school, or at least they used to when I was her age. I hear the rumble of the quake continuing. *God, is this ever going to stop?* Usually these things are like a few seconds of turbulence on a plane. This one's just not letting up, and the jolts are so strong.

"Dylan! Wake up!" I yell.

I hear the lamp in the corner crash to the floor. I step towards the doorway, slip my phone into my pajama pocket and press my hands against the sides of the door jamb as I stand underneath it to try to find my balance.

"Mommy!" Lily calls for me, and I can hear the panic in her voice growing. I keep my focus on the light in her room.

"Just hold onto the leg of the desk, honey. I'm coming!" I feel like everything's in slow motion, but moving so fast at the same time. It's not letting up.

"Babe! Are you ok?" Dylan shouts from our room. Finally, he's awake. Our bookshelf crashes down behind me, nearly grazing my back as I keep moving forward even though I haven't fully gotten my balance. I'm in the hallway and seeing that the picture frames are all slanted, and one of them has fallen onto the floor. Lily's crying, and it's taking forever for me to get to her.

"I'm ok! Be careful. There's glass everywhere!" I yell back and stumble toward Lily's room. My hands press against the wall, holding me up as the ground rolls underneath my feet. I'm on a roller coaster with no seatbelts. The air is a bit smoky now. Is something on fire? But it seems faint, so maybe it's far away in the neighborhood. I need to move fast and get to Lily. Why is everything in slow motion? My eyes catch tiny pieces of dust and paint chips. It's irritating my eyes and I can't blink it away. I see the wall is separating from the ceiling. The foundation of the house is shifting, and dirt is falling from where I never clean on top of the high shelves. This is not like any of the other quakes we've ever had!

I manage two steps forward and my foot falls out of the slipper. Why did I think slippers were a good idea as safety shoes for this kind of emergency? I arch back to get my foot into these ridiculous foot protectors, and I lose my balance again. Forget it. If I get cut, I get cut. I need to get to Lily. I make it four steps down the hallway, and stop in my tracks when I hear the mirror in the living room shatter. It's so ear-piercing, Lily's cries match it.

"Stay right there!" I yell. I can't keep my balance long enough to take even two steps forward. I'm inside a giant snow globe and whoever's holding it needs to put it down already. It's impossible to stand still.

I plant my left foot slightly forward and firmly onto the ground so that my other foot can stay back and help with balance. I press both of my hands against the hallway walls on either side of me as my body rides the tidal wave that this entire house has become. I can smell condiments that have fallen and broken open onto the kitchen floor: soy sauce, hot sauce, vinegar. Outside, people are shouting and car alarms are going off. The world is loud but muffled at the same time.

I hold my breath and let go of the wall for two seconds, and grab it again when the earth tests my balance. Maybe I can crawl to Lily's room. I crouch down. As my view of the ground bobs up and down, I see the hardwood floor is now covered in glass from every single picture frame we carefully hung along the hallway. I stand back up and Dylan's yelling behind me but I can't make out what he's saying. I turn my head to see him. The bookshelf is blocking our bedroom doorway. He's trying to move it out of the way but it's jammed. I turn my head away. I can't focus on anything right now except the light in Lily's room. I trip with every step through the hallway, but I'm inching forward. I don't hear her calling my name anymore, and my heart sinks. "Lillyyyy!" My throat is sore from screaming.

I finally make it through the noise and the smoky air to Lily's room. Where is she?!! Her once tidy room looks like it exploded. There are toys and books and pictures scattered everywhere. I go straight to her desk, which is what we'd practiced before. She's supposed to climb underneath, hold onto the leg of the desk with one hand and cover the back of her neck with the other. I'm trying to stay calm, but my heart is aching with fear and not knowing if she's ok.

"Lily!!" I yell desperately. I still can't see her. I'm out of my mind right now! I'm yelling at the top of my lungs. I'm kicking the books, toys and stuffed animals out of my way. I need to get to her. I drop to my knees. It's so hard to see the desk through all the dust in the air. I thrust forward and the standing lamp crashes down, hurling shattered glass across the hardwood floor and onto her shag lavender rug like confetti.

"Lily? Are you ok?!" Nothing. My heart's racing, and this feels so unreal. Images flash through my head of her sweet smile as she held up her unicorn paintings, and then switch to a vision of her crying hard, her face scared and helpless, and my panic messes with my imagination and creates images in my mind of my worst nightmare: of her face motionless, mouth partly open, skin gray with dust. Tears roll down my cheeks, and I'm frantically pushing my way through her room to get to her. Why isn't she saying anything?! The smoky air is making me insane! I'm so disoriented it's like I'm in another house and I have no idea where I'm going.

I bend down to let my hands find her. I feel small pieces of glass, I don't even care that they're pricking my hands, I feel her cozy fleece blanket and my heart warms up. She's ok. She has to be ok. But why can't I hear her? All I can hear is the rumbling of our house, things crashing down off shelves, and the unsteadiness of my heart. I keep holding my breath.

I let go of trying to focus my vision to find her, and let my hands feel the blanket and follow it as if it's a trail towards Lily. Is this her version of bread-crumbs? If it is, it's working. The floors are still rumbling underneath me. I can't believe this quake is still going. It's never lasted this long. I see a spotlight, and I imagine it's coming from her holding a flashlight inside the blanket.

"Lily!" I'm trying to pull the blanket aside, but she must have draped it over the chair and secured it with several books on the bottom, where it falls and meets the floor. She has created her own tent. How did she do all this? I move in closer and I can feel myself breathing again when I finally see her little feet. It looks like she'd done what we practiced, but she also pulled the chair in to create a tight and close space. I'm desperate to get to her. I pull the blanket aside, and see her sitting cross-legged, surrounded by every sin-gle pillow we've ever gotten her, and clutching Max the monkey with her ballerina music box in her lap.

"Lily! Oh my God! Thank God!" *I'm beside myself.* My heart and stomach are doing somersaults and tears are rolling down my cheeks. The ground is

moving underneath us, unsteady, rolling at times, with quick jolts every so often. The sounds are unreal; as if we're not even in our own home right now. This isn't how our home feels, how it moves, how it smells. I crawl into her tent with her, and I hold her and pull her close to me. She finally moves, climbing up and facing me, wrapping her arms around my waist like my little cub. She was a tiny baby the last time I held her like this.

"This feels like a very bouncy car ride, doesn't it?" I say to her.

I gotta figure out what the hell to do now. Alright, I can either try to get us out of here or stay right here under this desk. The smoke still seems like it's at a distance, so the house isn't burning down; maybe it's from down the street. If we move, something might fall on us and break our necks or flatten us like pancakes in two seconds. And they always say to stay underneath something sturdy. I'm taking the risk of keeping us right here.

Lily's looking up at me with wide eyes full of trust. This responsibility—being in charge of taking care of this little girl, this entire human—is something I've felt so differently about at various points in my life. This duty has made me feel overwhelmed, angry, freaked out, panicked, resentful, appreciative, motivated. But in this moment, as we sit in our Lily-made tent, holding onto each other as the world is crashing down outside and all around us, I am honored and know I'm exactly the person she needs to protect her and save her. She's loved and safe and I know how to do both with her right here, right now. I can't stop the ground from shaking, I can't stop it from jolting, I can't stop it from breaking and cracking underneath me, or keeping the walls from crashing down. But I can make sure that the invisible string between us is firm and strong and secure and something she knows will never be broken.

Above the wailing sirens and people scream-ing outside, I hear the loudest bang from what seems like the kitchen. Did the whole thing fall down? The cabinets! No way! I can see it in my mind's eye. All the dishes and glasses everywhere. I hear plates and glasses and Dylan's liquor bottles jumping off the shelves and bouncing onto the tiles. I just know that all the liquor bottles, goblets, and wine glasses Dylan spent hours organizing are now on the ground in pieces.

Lily's clinging onto me. We breathe together as we hear the crashing continue. I tuck her head into my chest, making sure we're both secure underneath her solid oak desk and that her neck is covered. "Let's hug and snuggle for a little bit," I tell her.

Lily nuzzles into me and I can feel her little hands squeezing my waist as tightly as she can. I feel a sting of fear in my upper chest and in my throat. For a split second, I imagine the roof caving in and collapsing onto us, where we cannot move. "We're going to be ok," I say to her, trying to reassure myself as well. I have no clue if I'm lying to her or to myself. I think of my exit strategy if that were to happen. I would cover her body with mine, creating a secure bridge over her.

She opens her ballerina music box. I breathe deeply and we start humming the melody of "Hero" as the pink ballerina twirls on her toes. Lily's grip loosens, but she doesn't unwrap her arms from around my waist. The shaking has stopped, but I know better than to think the quake is over. Now we just sit and wait for the aftershocks.

We wait and wait and wait, and there's still no aftershock. I check my phone. I have 40% battery power, but wi-fi isn't working. I'm nervous to even peek out of Lily's self-made tent. I like it in here. It's our retreat away from the scary world out there.

I have no idea what I'm going to see when I move the blanket. I have no idea if I'll be able to walk out of this room. Are we even alive right now? Is this another nightmare? Did we survive this? I've been through earthquakes since I was Lily's age, but those were all fives or less on the Richter Scale. This has to be a seven, or maybe an eight? No one could survive an eight! Wasn't the quake in Mexico City an eight, the one that killed hundreds of people?

Another tremendous jolt hits us and it's chilling. I thought we went through the worst of it already! But this aftershock is swinging us back and forth, and I can hardly hold onto Lily. Fire trucks and ambulances are wailing in the distance. I'm trying with all my might to keep my arms wrapped around her. I hear screams and crashes and bangs from all around the city.

I swear this is a movie. I want to shut it off and switch it to *Love Actually* or any rom-com. My body is numb and tense and hot and cold all at once. I don't want to die. I have so much more I need to do in this life. Lily needs to live her life. She can't die. Please, she can't die! I don't know who I'm talking to in my mind: myself, God, the universe?

The aftershock finally stops. I'm not moving. I know there's another one coming. There has to be. These are too strong.

Are my mom and brother alive? And Helen and Sarah? Are my patients ok? Am I at the epicenter, or are they getting it worse where they are? Are they feeling this at all? They have to be. This thing is crazier than anything I've ever gone through. I'm certain that if we ever get out of this alive, it's going to look like a war zone outside my front door.

The shaking starts again.

I want to get out of this bunker, but I know we're supposed to stay put under a secure surface. I need to get out of here. I need this thing to stop already. I can see past the blanket; the wall across from us has started leaning in. My heart is pounding so hard, I can hear it. I let Lily and me sink deeper into her desk, so we're one with it and she's completely hidden from this scary world. I try to think of anything I can that will get her mind to focus on something else.

"Can you look at your PJs and tell me what's on them?"

"Ice cream cones and teddy bears." She plays along as we brace ourselves for the next tremor. My palms are sweating so much, I swear they're dripping.

"What kind of ice cream?" I ask her.

"Chocolate, strawberry..." she continues as I look around to see what I can do if that wall comes down. Where can we run to? Or even worse, what if this desk gives out and can't be our shield? I can't think about that. It's going to hold. It's going to protect us.

I realize I haven't heard Dylan in a long time. Oh my God! How have I completely forgotten about him?

"*Dylan?*" I shout so loudly, I startle Lily.

Nothing. The shaking stops. Hopefully for the last time. Is he still in our room? Did he even hear me over the crashing sounds and the earth rumbling and car alarms going off outside? I don't hear fire trucks or ambulances anymore. Is the city dead? Is Dylan dead? We're on the brink of death, and my whole existence for the last seven years has been living for him and thinking about him and doing things according to him, and running things by him. "*Dylan*?!" I yell again, desperate for my voice to pierce through the chaos inside and outside our home.

Nothing.

"Dylan!" I try again, and again and again. Nothing.

Oh my God. I'm numb, even with that thought going through my mind. This man I fell in love with, shared a life with, how can I feel numb? How is that possible? I try again, though this time my volume doesn't reach the level it had before.

"Dylan?!"

"Daddy!" Lily shouts.

The earth starts moving underneath us again. *Here we go.* I hold Lily tightly. This aftershock is softer; it's a slow rocking and bouncing, as if I'm sitting in a bouncy house and kids are jumping around me. Lily's little hands are squeezing my back.

I have to distract her. "How many teddy bears are on your PJs?" I ask Lily, praying she keeps playing along with my game. It's helping her as much as it's helping me.

"One, two, three, four..." She focuses on each one as she keeps counting. Thank God I bought the ones with tons of tiny teddy bears.

The shaking stops. We both freeze, not trusting that it's over. She looks up at me. I kiss her on the head, nervous.

I look up. It's as if someone drew a crooked line on the wall starting in the corner and ripped the wall apart, and I swear I can see into the bathroom. *Oh my God, what if the ceiling comes down on us?* My mind is calculating exits and escape routes blindingly fast, in ways I've never even thought about this house.

If I could get us to the kitchen, that table over there wouldn't be any better than this desk we're under right now. The bathroom's not an option. Maybe the closet, where it's completely enclosed? But there's zero protection in there. If we manage to climb out this bedroom window and actually make it out to the side yard, that trellis might as well be as useful as a bedsheet as far as protection.

The most mind-blowing crash fills the entire house, followed by a series of booms. I can only see about two feet ahead of me. Everything is dark. Something must have landed on the roof and demolished the house. The entire structure seems to have caved in, and Lily's room is now the size of this desk. All my muscles tighten. I am her shelter. I cover her with my entire body and my little cub is defenseless but for some possibly delusional reason, I feel she's safe with me.

"Mommy, I'm scared," Lily's trying to catch her breath as her cry emerges.

"It's ok, honey. It's almost over."

Courage, strength, hope. Courage, strength, hope. It's a loop running in my mind. I'm just watching those words scroll across a silent screen. *Alright*, I tell myself, *when I can count for four straight minutes, I'll try to get us out of here.*

Though the sounds of crashing, banging, car alarms, and screams continue around us, we settle back into our familiar zone. I hold her tightly with my left arm, and she takes my index finger and brings it up to her face. I trace her features ever so slowly. My fingertip outlines her hairline, goes across each of her eyebrows, along her eyelashes, down the bridge of her nose, and along her puffy cheeks. I trace the outline of her top lip and she puckers her lips and kisses my fingertip. Amidst this chaos, she's pure love.

Another aftershock comes. This one is strong. The jolts are not stopping. I can't see the ceiling or the walls now. I can't even see her bed. I want to get out of here, but I'm not risking it just yet. We need to stay in place. If the rest of the roof falls in, it will kill us for sure. It has to be, what, at least a couple of tons? A few hundred pounds? I'm terrible at this stuff. Can a solid oak desk survive that kind of impact?

I'm completely powerless. The only exit route that's an option is the one we're in now: to sit here under Lily's desk, and ride it out. My arms are cramping from squeezing her tight for so long, but I can't loosen my grip. Tears mixed in dust sting my eyes, and my arms have goosebumps as I'm immersed in this responsibility. She can't die. I can't die. I find myself drifting into a deep sleep.

*　　　*　　　*　　　*

"Hey!" a man's voice shouts. "Over here!"

I wake up to jumbled sounds above me. It takes every ounce of energy I have to pry open my eyes. They're stuck together with residue from tears and dust and gunk. Did this really happen? Was that just another one of my nightmares? I feel Lily still nuzzled into me in her self-made tent. It all feels so eerie. Did we survive this thing? I must have been passed out for several hours.

The rescuing stranger lifts broken sections of the ceiling, or maybe it's the wall, that's have crashed down on us, and the tiny dark space brightens. By the grace of God, the solid oak desk broke the fall of the bedroom wall, which has split into pieces. I guess it was a smart purchase after all.

I look down and see Lily's in the same position I remember her in when the world came crashing down on us. She's nestled into me, her ballerina music box is still open, and her pink ballerina is still twirling to "Hero." I feel a little dizzy. My back and arms are sore from staying in this fixed position.

The man standing above us persists and eventually removes all obstruction blocking the open air, trying to free us from our bunker. A slight breeze tingles my skin. There are distant screams, muffled chatter and sounds of people near and far.

I'm disoriented, as if I'm on another planet. I'm starving; my body feels weak and like it's been eating itself. I can hear my stomach growling.

I need to get a grip on reality. I look at my right hand, spread my fingers, stretch out my palm and hear little cracks as my index finger, pinky, and thumb extend outward. I gasp when it hits me that Lily is totally still. Her mouth is partly open and it looks like she's not breathing. Panic visits me. I place my left hand on Lily's little rib cage for any indication of breathing. Relief washes over me when I see my hand rise and fall with the subtle movements of her back. My eyes find hers, which are still closed, but I can see she's in REM sleep as her eyes are darting back and forth underneath her eyelids. The sun's spotlight is shining down onto her. She looks so peaceful, and there's a glow on her cheeks. Her eyelashes look like miniature fans. Looking at this face, one would never know the nightmare we've been through. The man who's here to rescue us is still standing overhead. He stretches his arm out.

"Lady, grab my hand!" He shouts.

I'm frozen, in complete denial about what's happening. We make eye contact, which soothes me, as I convince myself that this must be a sign that at least he must think my face looks like I'm not yet ready to be buried.

I reach for his hand, but I can't move. My legs and butt are completely stiff and cramping from being in the same position for hours on end. But that's not why I'm stuck. My 40-pound angel is glued to my sweat-soaked body. I bring my hand back down.

"Lily, honey! Wake up, please!" I shout and peel her away from me, touching her face and begging her to open her eyes. I know she's alive, but—I just need to know she's alive.

I pat her back, and yell even louder this time, "Lily, c'mon! Wake up!"

She hums and flutters her eyes. Her neck muscles pop as she stretches, wiggles and unglues herself from me.   "Mommy?" She says softly.

"Oh, thank God!" I exhale and squeeze her in a tight hug. My little angel. Her music box closes and the sounds above us leak into our space.

"Lady! C'mon! Grab my hand!" It sounds like he's not only losing his voice, but also his patience with me. Wow, how long have I been making this guy wait to save our lives? The reality that I can finally get the heck out of here hits me. He's somehow managed to get his upper body far enough into our little bunker. It seems like someone is behind him holding his legs so he doesn't fall in. I imagine this is what those guys Sarah hooks up with look like—broad shoulders, strong hands. I feel about twenty years younger in his arms, and he lifts Lily and me in one fell swoop.

"You ladies are real lucky, ya know that? We've been searching over here for hours. Someone heard the sounds of that little music box coming from under there. We thought there were no survivors in this house." He gets to his feet, still holding on to us. He looks less annoyed than he sounds. Maybe he just has a deep voice.

He helps us both stand up. "You ready to see somethin' you won't believe?"

I was right. There was another guy holding his legs so he could reach us, under the collapsed roof that had trapped us. My vulnerability returns when I see and hear a small crowd of people cheering.

"It's pretty magical," he adds. If it were any other day, I would've given the guy a disapproving mom look and told him to watch his language around my kid. But today, I'll keep the stick out of my ass for once. I hear distant screams, muffled chatter and sounds of people near and far.

"Magical?" Lily asks. That's all she needs to get her adrenaline boost. She stands up. Her lashes flutter and her brown eyes scan her surroundings.

"Mommy! It *is* magic!"

I feel the blood drain from my face as I get up. "I really need to get us food," I say to the guy.

"Alright, lady. I'm sorry but you're on your own from here," he says and climbs down the side of the rubble pile that was once our home. He's off with some other people to continue their rescue mission.

I pull myself up off the ground, and Lily jumps up and down. "Mommy, look!" I find myself in both awe and confusion.

Eyes wide and jaws hanging open, Lily and I look around. What we see doesn't look like magic to me. This is eerie, it's chaos, it's confusing. Our entire neighborhood is demolished, houses are flattened, fires are burning in the distance. I can't recognize a single thing. We're not in our house. We're not in anything. We're outside! We lost our entire house!

My eyes try their best to take in what's around us. The bright sun is heating my skin. The baby blue skies calm me as I'm trying to figure out this Twilight Zone I'm in. It looks like we're floating on a tiny piece of land.

This

    is

        unreal.

I can't quite make out what's happened. Is my entire neighborhood one little island? There's my hot neighbor's house—across from us, with about a hundred yards of ocean water between us! I lift my gaze and take in this strange and scary, yet intriguing, new world. I feel like I'm standing on a boat in the middle of the ocean, but I'm where Lily's bedroom used to be.

People are moving in slow motion, lifting large objects out of the way together; others are yelling for each other, and still others are crying. Pieces of wood are strewn across the ground, street lights and electric poles are asleep on the broken concrete, just as exhausted as the rest of us. Did the quake break off the California coastline? It must have been along the San Andreas Fault! We used to joke about it, but never in a million years would any of us have imagined it would become a reality.

There's a stillness in the air as I'm digesting this new life. It's an eerie moment as my perception adjusts to this surreal movie scene. What day is it? It feels like months have passed, or maybe I'm on The Truman Show. Or maybe I need anti-psychotic meds like Sarah suggested.

Lily's footsteps crunch the rubble as she steps closer to me. I take her hand and I'm ready to console her tears, to comfort her panic, to soothe her worries. But there's no need. She's fine. She's calm, looking around at everything, taking it all in just like I am. We probably look like two little kids at a zoo. But there are no lions, tigers or bears. In their place are houses we don't recognize anymore, the ones we used to walk by. Ocean water surrounds us - a whole new life.

I keep expecting to see sailboats, surfers or paddle-boarders floating on the water around us, just like we do every day at this time of year, but there's not one in sight. Cars are trapped underneath light poles, and the earth is broken up in such strange ways. I'm used to the sidewalks in the neighborhood being uneven and a bit broken from mini-quakes we had back when I was in elementary school, and from the large trees' roots proving that nature can push through man-made concrete. But this is an entirely new dimension.

The fog is beginning to clear, and it's like I'm at Universal Studios and we're standing in a lot amongst actors filming a movie, doing action scenes in various locations around us. I want to stay in my cozy little Lily bubble, before I risk jumping out there with the rest of them. "Let's find our socks and shoes."

Lily still has her socks on from the night before. That gives us one less thing to search for. She immediately finds her unicorn sneakers. They still have the iridescent shine on the edges. She slips her foot in, and pulls up the mini wings on the end of the zipper that runs along the outside of the sneaker. She does the same with her other foot and stands up again.

I lean over and kiss the top of her head. The scent of her shampoo is now gone, and instead I catch a whiff of dust and oil and sweat. "Ok, my turn!" I say. I point to my dust-covered feet. "Let's see if we can find my shoes in this haystack." I see what used to be our bathtub. We head towards our phantom bathroom, and I try to follow the map in my mind to remember how far the master bedroom was from there.

I swear, my feet are catching every sharp edge underneath them right now. Damn, that hurts! I can already envision myself sitting with my foot up and a pair of tweezers at some point, performing self-surgery to remove God knows what from my skin. I try to stay on my toes, and wish I wasn't so sensitive, and that I could be more like my neighbors next door who go barefoot every day of their lives.

Before this disaster, when I would walk from my door to the beach, I would never leave home without my flip-flops. The hot sand would be unbearable for the few hundred steps it took me to reach the water.

"I see your shoe rack, Mommy!" Lily's already climbed up and over the fallen dresser laying on the ground and is pulling out shoes, trying to find matching pairs.

"Be careful," I say. For what? I don't know.

Two white matching sneakers. It's unbelievable how easy that was. Now, it'll be a miracle if I can find my socks. I see my dresser. The drawers are smashed in and look like crooked teeth. I press the palm of my hand against the top of the dresser, and let my other hand curve underneath the drawer handle to pull it. It's jammed shut. I pull again, more forcefully this time. I push my foot against the base of the dresser in an attempt to gain more leverage. Am I really straining all my muscles for some socks right now? This is so bizarre. I pull hard against the handle, and it rips off, sending me tumbling backward to the ground. "Seriously?" I shout.

Lily's laughing and mimicking me. "Seriously?" she says. I have to admit, the whole thing is pretty ridiculous, and I can't help but join her. I reach over and tickle her tummy. She's giggling and tickling me back. I hate being tickled, but I tolerate it from her. Who can resist those contagious giggles?

"Ok, ok, ok," I say, begging her to let up. She gives me a break, and we both lay flat on our backs, catching our breath, looking up at the sky. It's truly beautiful. It's hard to believe what's going on right now. We lost our home; everyone we know did. We lost our neighborhood, and maybe our city. Did Los Angeles really break off at the San Andreas Fault? I really wish I could Google this right now.

A seagull caws and soars across the blue sky overhead. I return to reality and hear the sounds of people around us trying to salvage and repair what's theirs. I stand up and attempt the sock challenge again. I consider for a split second that I could just wear my sneakers without socks. One more try, and if I can't get into this damn drawer, I'll just have to deal with that.

I see that the bottom drawer is still intact and not wedged in like the top drawer. If I can wiggle the bottom drawer a bit and get it out, I'll be able to reach up from underneath and reach the drawer above, pull that one towards me and remove it. Then I can get my precious socks. It goes exactly as planned, and the dopamine rush is pretty rewarding. I put on clean socks, along with my sneakers, and voila!

"Where's Daddy?" Lily asks. Oh my God, how have I not thought the same thing? What's wrong with me? I squint as the sun beats down on us. I can feel the almost unnoticeable swaying of the ground underneath me. How am I so numb right now? I remember feeling this during the quake, and it's still surprising me. I do wonder where he is or how he is, but I'm not panicked and overly consumed by everything that is him, like I have been for the last seven years.

I catch glimpses of people in clusters on their own missions. We're all trying to figure this out, but it feels like we're strangely connected and in this together. I lead Lily on a search for any sign of Dylan.

I see Sally who lives in the blue house down the street. "Hey, Jelina! You guys ok?" she shouts from across the way.

"We're looking for Dylan!" I shout back.

She walks towards us. "Oh! He had a concussion and was taken that way a few hours ago," Sally points to the left of us.

"Thank you so much!" I say to her as she reaches us.

"Want me to go with you guys?" She asks.

"Yeah! Please. This is all so crazy!" I respond.

We begin walking in the direction she told us.

I look up at the sun, and think about how fast that thing's going to move—it'll be dark before we know it. We'll need light. I haven't even checked my phone until this moment. There's no way there's reception. I pull it out of my pocket, and click the home button. Dead. How are we going to do this? We're starting from scratch. Water, food, electricity? Where are we going to sleep? We're in survival mode.

I look around at all the rubble and homes in shambles, and the image of my dream retreat that I've drawn on countless napkin flashes in front of me. I can see it all. Tents with signs, pathways to each of them, the fire pit in the middle, paddle-boards hanging on racks, and people painting and playing guitar. I see it all clearly.

My heart sinks when my eyes try to find Sunkissed Café. "Natalia," I whisper. A tear escapes my eye as I imagine the worst. *She has to be ok. She's strong. We'll find her! This is so hard.* I wipe the tears from my eyes.

"Ok, what can I help with?" Sally shakes me out of my fear-trance.

"Can you get as many people to gather flashlights, food, blankets, and as many water bottles as you can find?" I'm scared, and I don't know what I'm doing. "Let's all meet back at the Magic Sand Castle house before sundown." The words just spill out of my mouth.

"Where?" She's perplexed.

"Over there." Lily says and points down the block, where a shiny silver door smiles back at us. "That's where the Magic Sand Castle house used to be!" She's so assertive and the fact that she's even jumping in and speaking to another human being is blowing me away. Who is this kid? My heart warms with delight.

"You got it," Sally responds. I'm shocked by how grateful she seems to receive my command.

I have to get back to my mission with Lily. We need to find her dad. I catch Lily's expression. She seems concerned, but for the first time in her four years on this planet, I can see confidence in her eyes. I like this look. It suits her well. I keep a tight grasp on her hand as we climb over sheet metal and broken walls.

"This way!" I shout.

Dear God, please tell me he's ok. Just don't do this to her. Lily needs her father. It's so easy to die. We work so hard and go through such pain and sorrow, studying hard and paying bills, and then we die—just like that. No replay. Simply game over.

"I'm sure he's helping people or maybe he got tired and he's sleeping. Let's look for some water and something to eat until we find him," I say, praying we'll hear him any moment now. I'm panicked that we'll find him in the worst way imaginable. I just can't fathom her seeing that. I attempt to distract her so that I can screen for any dead bodies before she discovers them.

"But what if he's over this way, Mommy?" she says, pointing in the direction we were headed before. Lily's too smart for me to get away with these casual distractions like I could when she was a toddler. With her hand still clasped in mine, I speed-walk us in the opposite direction. She has to pick up her pace to run to keep up with me. We hike across what used to be our suburban neighborhood.

"Why are we going this way?" she asks. Before I can come up with some elaborate answer as I try to pull her away from a possible PTSD trap—only to fail miserably—nature rescues me.

Lily releases my hand. I slow down as I see a butterfly fluttering her red wings around us. Lily's eyes are fixated on every flip and turn it makes. I feel the tension in my shoulders loosen as I'm watching the two of them dancing together. They're in their own little world. I'm so drawn to this sweet scene that I'm not paying attention to where I'm walking. Her red butterfly. I smile to myself.

My foot catches on a large white strip of what looks like the fence from the neighbor's yard three houses down. It's definitely their fence, because I also see their silver door, which always intrigued me when Lily and I would go for walks. Her favorite Magic Sand Castle House, because it was steps from the sand that led to the beach. I swear, the light from the ocean water would hit the silver door in such a way that she was right. It was glowing.

Now, it's blended in with the rest of us. Amidst all the rubble, it's impossible to tell where the Magic Sand Castle ends and where the other homes begin. We're all one.

A blurry figure comes barreling through the crowd out of nowhere. His face is beet red, but I'm blind from exhaustion.

"*Daddy!*!" Lily shouts. She runs over to Dylan, who's running towards us about fifty feet away.

He catches her as she jumps onto him. Dylan's holding her up; she's got her legs wrapped around his waist and her arms are tight around his neck. They're both in their own bubble of bliss.

"I'm a tree. You can climb me," Dylan says, and Lily giggles and squeals. He squats down, and lowers them both onto the grass. He's sitting cross-legged and Lily's cuddling up against him.

I see him so differently now. He's no longer my husband. He's Lily's Dad. "I'm glad you're ok," I say.

"Yeah," he says.

I feel as though I've been in a washing machine, punched and thrown and caught and retrieved. My head is spinning. I don't even know which way is up. Everything I've ever known is gone. Who I was is gone. I'm going to be a divorced woman now. My entire neighborhood has been demolished. I'm starting from scratch. Do I still do therapy? How do I make sure Lily still gets everything she needs? Do we have electricity, and clean water to drink? Am I ever going to see my family and friends again? I'm nervous, but surprisingly calm at the same time.

Lying on the grass, Natalia's face floats into my mind. My heart stings a little. I'm not ready to think about what's happened with her. I'm going to keep her right here in my heart with me, just as she has been since the moment I met her in that accident on Ocean Avenue. When there was an Ocean Avenue.

I take a breath of fresh air, close my eyes and transport myself to our sound bath ecstasy, the moment she walked up to my car, when she came up behind me and wrapped her arms around my chest, and our Santa Monica roller coaster ride, walking hand in hand talking about anything and everything. I never thought I'd say this, but thank God for that accident. It saved my life. She came into my life for a reason, and made me feel alive.

I close my eyes and take in a deep breath, inhale her love, and open my eyes as I exhale, letting my gaze rest on the soft sky and gentle clouds. The sky says *hello*, as it always does. That's the one thing I've been able to count on in my life. No matter what's going on, I can always look up at the sky and she's there for me.

My brain's trying to make sense of this new reality. I sit here, on the path that used to lead to Surfer's Park, looking out at the ocean water. Lily's telling Dylan the play-by-play of our rescue mission.

My arms are resting on my knees. The sunlight is hitting the surface of the water in such a special way. I can't take my eyes off of this beautiful live painting. An artist has magically taken a thick paintbrush and created long wavy strokes of dark blues and turquoise in front of me. He's painted thin white borders along the tips of the waves where they splash against the curves of the land. And he's now sprinkling glitter from his fingertips and spreading them across the waves. They are a sea of diamonds.

I see a vision of my six-year-old inner child from my dreams. She's sitting near the edge of the water, cross legged, with her notebook in her lap. All my life, I've been letting her down. I remember writing letters and thoughts in my notebooks. I have no clue to whom I was writing, but I do know writing is where I feel safe and hopeful in a world where I felt alone and lost.

I've been overworking my inner child, and pushing her to the limits, exhausting her until she's burnt out. I haven't been paying attention to her, and I've even forgotten about her. I've put everyone else's needs—especially Dylan's—before hers. I haven't asked for help, or let anyone help her. I've felt ashamed of her, and I've neglected her, treating her the same way she was treated as a child. I don't give her any time or attention; letting her get neglected and traumatized and taken advantage of; being a victim, I tell her she's not good enough and not beautiful, that she's stuck with repeated self-talk and criticism. I've shamed her with hateful messages and images in my mind that haunted meme with hallucinations.

But she's been with me all along. She's within me. She *is* me. It's my job to protect her, and I promise to do that from here on out.

We all get up off the ground to walk back towards the house—or what was our house. A folded piece of paper falls out of Lily's pajama pocket. "What's this?" I ask her, and grab it.

"That's my Sketch," she says.

I unfold the little paper and a surge of electricity moves through my veins. "Your island sketch," I whisper. I look up at my surroundings. Crumbled buildings surround us, flattened homes, and ocean water separates us from our neighbors down the block.

We're on that island now. How is this possible? It's all so surreal. I'm going to wake up at any time.

Chapter Fifteen:

Aftermath (June 21, 2028)

It's been five years since the day our lives changed forever. Natalia was never found after the earthquake. I kept looking for months and months. I see visions of her in my daydreams.

I exhale, and settle into my hammock, adjust the pillows so they're just right, draw a blanket over my legs and start scrolling through my phone. I pull up the detailed news report that was published at 5 a.m. this morning, giving us answers to questions we've been stirring around since that fateful day.

We've all been hungry for this kind of infor-mation, sitting with the surreal feeling in our stomachs that the landscape of Los Angeles has completely transformed, and that this isn't all just some strange dream. What's kept me dumbfounded is that my name is in this news story. Yes, *me*! I opened the news report three hours ago, and I can't even count how many times I've read it since then. Needless to say, I have pretty much memorized this thing by now. I'm still looking for Natalia's name to magically appear no matter how many times I read this.

CNN News Article - June 21, 2028: San Andreas Island, A Community Born Beyond California's Wildest Dreams

Five years ago on this day, at 5:30 a.m., the San Andreas Earthquake jolted Southern Californians at a magnitude of 9.7 on the Richter Scale and a maximum Mercalli intensity of XI (Extreme). In one of the most unprecedented natural disasters in modern history, the coast of Santa Monica was split off into what's now been named San Andreas Island, separated by a two-mile-wide sandbar.

The epicenter was in the city of Santa Monica and lasted one minute and fourteen seconds, with six aftershocks averaging a magnitude of 5 on the Richter Scale. The heartbreaking death toll numbered 5,140 people, and over 200,000 others became homeless or displaced from their residences. Thousands fled the city and headed north or out of state.

Heart-wrenching screams could be heard from people drowning in the water as the earth split open at the San Andreas Fault Line. Families were torn apart and were without contact, not knowing who was dead or alive.

The 405 and 101 Freeways collapsed. Three hundred tons of concrete slammed down on the road below, as rush hour traffic was brewing, smashing pedestrians and killing drivers on their way to work, above and underneath the overpasses. Shaking was felt as far inland as Las Vegas.

Devastating fires soon broke out in the city and lasted for several days. Thousands of homes were dismantled. Even firefighters were speechless.

A volatile mix of fire and water spread throughout the city, and much of the destruction was caused by the out-of-control flames. People were trapped inside homes and buildings for days. Some were never rescued, and some were never found due to the fires decimating the structures they were in.

Portable generators saved thousands of lives, giving construction workers light to work on the city 24/7. Television crews were able to do their jobs and broadcast the reality of the crisis to the world, causing help to arrive faster than it might have otherwise.

Out of the 19 schools in Santa Monica, only two are still standing. For weeks, it was not uncommon to see people being carried away on stretchers to receive medical care. People were getting medical treatment right on the streets.

Hospitals were incapable of providing adequate care for the overflow of patients, medicine and prescriptions ran out, and most homes had no electricity or clean water for many weeks. Moans could be heard throughout the city from people not yet rescued.

Many residents were given only a few minutes to get their belongings and get out of their homes. So many people lost everything they knew. Pets, wedding photos, and everything else was burned or destroyed. People were not able to evacuate in time, and countless family members were not able to get to their loved ones because of blocked roads and no operating phones.

It has taken multi billion dollar budgets to rebuild Santa Monica into what it is today. Still, five years later, thousands of makeshift tents sprawl throughout the city.

Although buildings and homes were engineered to abide by earthquake codes, and structures were retrofitted with heavy steel beams and massive strips of rubber to absorb the seismic shock to roll the buildings like wheels, it was impossible for anyone to have been prepared for this extraordinary quake. Residents who were prepared had to survive for the first five consecutive days on their own non-perishable food and stored gallons of water, were instructed to shut off their gas, and had no technology, no wifi, no landlines, and no electricity.

Tongva Park, named after the first inhabitants of this beach city, has undergone a complete rebirth and renovation. The most desirable real estate homes in Southern California were demolished in a minute and fourteen seconds.

The top seismologists at Stanford University have been conducting extensive research as to how San Andreas Island was created as a result of this quake, particularly with California being on a strike-slip fault line.

According to their findings, California sits on two tectonic plates, the Pacific Plate and the North American Plate. The San Andreas Fault Line separates the two plates and runs down the middle of California. This 800-mile crack is where the two massive tectonic plates meet. They are constantly moving past one another, which in essence means that Los Angeles migrates north a few inches each year.

In five to ten million years, Los Angeles will have travelled north and will be located right next to San Francisco.

Thrust faults differ from strike-slip faults in that the tectonic plates bend and don't slide past one another, but rather collide head on. What this means for California residents is that over eons, the constant banging where the plates meet has created small cracks which are wedged on top of each other, resulting in the creation of mountains on the earth's surface.

Mountains have created all of California's beautiful scenery, provided water sources and scattered valleys across the Los Angeles Basin.

In the San Andreas Earthquake, the plates were sliding past one another, and the grinding produced the seismic wave (an earthquake). The significant length of the San Andreas Fault in the earth's surface was what caused this Extreme intensity 9.7 magnitude quake and its massive separation into what appears to be an island, connected underwater by a two-mile sandbar.

The streets of Santa Monica have remained in their original rectangular grid, while those streets that have been built on San Andreas Island are circular, with three main diagonal roads intersecting them to make it easier to get across the island.

The late William James, a prominent psychologist at the turn of the 20th Century, once published his observations about another historical event: the 1906 San Francisco earthquake. His words are very much applicable to what Californians experienced with the 2023 San Andreas Quake.

He wrote, "The first of these was the rapidity of the improvisation of order out of chaos… the second thing that struck me was the universal equanimity."

Southern Californians pulled together in the rubble. The President declared the San Andreas Earthquake a state of emergency, and sent United States military troops across hundreds of miles throughout the city of Los Angeles on search and rescue missions, and to provide relief and support.

International aid showed up from far and wide. Our neighbors in Canada and Mexico arrived with medical supplies and food immediately. U.S. allies delivered assistance from across the Pacific Ocean, with Australia flying in natural products to build huts early on to provide temporary shelter, and Japan aiding with their technologically advanced military support.

New investors were brought in from out of state and internationally to reconstruct residential and commercial properties for hundreds of miles from the city of Santa Monica and all across Los Angeles County.

Despite the widespread support, many survivors were still forced to rebuild on their own. Thousands became volunteers who stepped in to help and go on searches, and they continue to volunteer their services two years later, reconstructing the city and this new way of life.

This devastating earthquake gave birth to the spiritual healing retreat that is known today as San Andreas Island Retreat. A Southern California native named Jelina King, a psychotherapist and single mother, spearheaded the transformation of this tiny but mighty piece of land into an island retreat.

"I was watching people die everyday, and I just couldn't sit back and do nothing," King said. "We've preserved and enhanced the original tents that were constructed two years ago, and situated them on the circular roads, so there is a constant feeling of unity between us.

"We have mindfulness hikes and runs daily, meditation on paddle boards on the water, and have three specialized rooms. The Raw Room is where healing and spiritual work happens like therapy and yoga. Counseling is available for every single person who wants it. The Focus Room is a very structured and

quiet space where people meditate and are guided to work on their writing and other projects without distractions, and the Nourish Room is where we eat meals together. It was inspired by my experience as a therapist in various treatment settings, and provides all the benefits of an addiction treatment center, but available to anyone and everyone.

"Boat taxis travel from the two docks on San Andreas Island to the new coast of Santa Monica. They serve two purposes: transporting people to and fro, and providing ocean and beach cleanup. There are sections of the sandbar where people can walk all the way across, with the assistance of thick ropes that have been securely mounted, stretching from the mainland to the island.

"The pain and fear snapped me into action, like dying in my marriage. My whole world stopped and I had to focus on my daughter and our survival. My life as I knew it fell apart and is coming back together in a special and meaningful way. I got a second chance at solace.

"This quake and island have been a rebirth in every way. The physical, emotional and life-changing earthquake ironically shook me to my core while rebuilding and strengthening this very same core right at its roots. Everything in and out of me was uplifted *from the ground, turned upside down, and shaken of all its leaves, leaving room for new fruit. All living and physical things were changed forever.*

"It is the earthquake that changed this Los Angeles landscape and created our new mountains to climb. Thus, from all the shaking and destruction came those fresh and much needed paths. The split in California helped us realize the splits within all of us and in our own lives, and for all to come together, much like the destruction and rebuilding after the 2023 earthquake.

"We must be mindful of our two Californias within each and every one of us. Whatever grief or life change we go through. We must find compassion for ourselves and everyone, as one never knows when your own 'stable' land might be split into two. The sounds of the earthquake from the core of the earth, are what we all sound like in our own core.

"What do we feel, look, and sound like when we have an earthquake? We all have them. We were living on this inevitable earthquake territory, and none of us were prepared for this.

"No one teaches us how to deal with nor prepare for our own life quakes, or how to deal with our lava when it comes out. We all truly reflect nature. Our sun shines, our darkness dampens, tornadoes swallow

us up and spit us out, quakes tear us down and rebuild us.

"This quake represented something different for each and every one of us. For me, it represented the divorce in my own life. San Andreas Island Retreat represents my recovery and renaissance."

Chapter Sixteen:

Wildest Dreams

Lily and I are standing parallel to each other on our yoga mats facing a group of about 30 yogis this late morning. We have the typical mix of ages, ranging from seven to 77. Lily speaks into the tiny microphone on her headset and guides the group through a Vinyasa Flow. I remain standing, taking in the moment, as I let her lead the groups. This nine-year-old is remarkable.

A warm ocean breeze blends with the sunlight, warming our island hut to the perfect temperature. It seems like it was just yesterday when the very ground we're standing on was one of the countless demolished homes from the quake. I still look around sometimes and think it's all a dream - both my physical surroundings on the island and my internal state of calm and emotional balance.

I gaze at all the people in our yoga class today. Helen and Sarah are towards the center in their usual spots, with Kyle and Luke beside them. I'm getting used to seeing Sarah in maternity mode. She's maneuvering around her pregnant belly as she holds her poses.

I still can't believe she's about to be a mom. She and Luke are going to be incredible parents, but I will always see her as the wild and free sex-crazed one with blue streaks in her hair. I look out past the crowd through our open air hut that we all helped build together after the quake. We recently had tremendous gifts from anonymous donors who I imagine dedicate their lives to fighting climate change. They donated floor to ceiling sliding glass doors around the entire room, and installed solar panel lighting systems for the entire island, and set up vertical farming throughout.

I can see the neighborhood where my mom and brother's family live now, and I feel comforted. My eyes then land on the taxi boats. They run every half hour around the clock between the new Santa Monica coast and San Andreas Island. To believe Los Angeles would ever have split off at the San Andreas

Fault, or that I'd be co-leading a yoga class with Lily in our island retreat, is all beyond my wildest dreams.

We decided to call this room we're in the Raw Room, where we have yoga classes, group therapy, art therapy and music. It's open 24/7, 365 days a year for anyone who wants to connect or release. People come when they're in all kinds of states: bored, lonely, depressed after a breakup, adjusting to a newly sober lifestyle. The smaller hut south of this one is the Focus Room, and it's set up as a quiet space where people can be productive, meditate, write, or read. And just up the road on the north side, is the Nourish Room. This is our charming café where people can select their own herbs from our very own Surfer's Garden, and organic food is brought over from the mainland about twice a day.

Zero 7 is playing through the speakers. In unison, Lily and I place our right heels up against the highest points on the inside of our left thighs. When we find balance with our left feet planted on the ground, we sweep our arms up and press our hands together for a tall tree pose. I smile to myself as I hear her guiding the group, and see the crowd following her instructions. My heart tingles with love and pride.

"Focus on your breath, and let go of everything happening outside of this room and this very moment," she says. I don't hear a trace of insecurity in her voice as she transitions the group into inversions. We release our tree pose, and I get down onto the mat on my hands and knees. Lily watches me as a reminder about proper form.

"Now, everyone here can do this next pose, even if it's your first time," she says as she follows my lead, getting onto her mat, still parallel to me. "It's now or never," she says as she looks at me and smiles. "Relax for a bit, and just watch me so you'll know what to do. You're going to start in a hands and knees position, and clasp your hands together with your forearms flat against the mat. Laying your head down to the mat against your hands, then move your hands back, placing them in the spots where your elbows were just resting." She peeks over at me. I move forward and she follows my lead.

She continues to speak to the group. "Let your fingertips press down, feeling like frog hands gripping into your mat. Now walk your feet towards you, and slowly shift your weight to your fingertips for balance like you would with your feet and toes if you were standing up. And lift your legs off the floor one at a time, resting your knees on your elbows. Then take your time and straighten your legs as you lift them straight up above you."

I smile as I watch her focused expression, following her own instructions carefully. She pulls herself up into an almost fully straight headstand. She's getting better each time. It's so endearing how I can feel that she truly cares about being able to teach every single person in this room how to do a headstand. We hold our pose for a few more seconds and then I hear some applause. I don't blame them. How can they not cherish this girl?

Lily releases her pose at the same time as me. I walk around the room, assisting some group members with positioning and balance as needed. I make eye contact with Lily and wave my hand upwards by my throat gesturing a breath. She reads my cue perfectly. "Remember to breathe," she tells the crowd. "Slowly inhale relaxation, and exhale tension."

They're following her instructions. One after the other, I see headstands springing up like tall blades of grass throughout the room.

Lily and I make eye contact again over the sea of people, and I draw the letter "S" in the air for her. She smiles. It's her favorite part. She sits cross-legged on her mat, with her hands relaxed on her knees. "Alright, everyone. It's time for the best part of our class." The group knows what this means by now, and they breathe a sigh of relief. "Lay down, settle in and get comfortable in Savasana pose."

I remain standing and float by the rows of colorful yoga mats, closing the group with a guided meditation. A sea of yogis lay flat in pin drop silence for ten minutes.

I tap the chime. "Take one last deep inhale, breathing in relaxation," I say and follow my own instructions, "and exhale, releasing tension."

The entire room breathes out in unison, wiggling out of their Savasana meditation poses. The crinkling sounds of feet pressing on the hardwood flooring, as people get up from their mats. The energy in the room shifts from quiet synchronicity to spontaneous movement, laughter and chatter.

I pull out the neon yellow Post-It I scribbled on before class.

"Just a reminder guys, before you head out: at noon we will be meeting in the small garden just outside the Nourish kitchen to do some planting and gathering for today's lunch." I stretch my arm out towards the back wall. "And we'll be guided by two extraordinary guest chefs today."

Their introduction is drowned out by everyone's cheers and whistles as they look at the back of the class. Helen and Kyle are hand in hand, and smile and nod to the crowd.

"We'll try to make you proud, J!" Helen calls to me. They got married last winter and travel the world, visiting schools and transforming cafeterias into food gardens where they teach kids to plant their own meals and learn mindful eating skills to combat childhood obesity. I love that my brother married one of my favorite people in the world. And when they're in town, I do my best to snag them to share their wisdom in the Nourish kitchen with us.

"Thank you, guys!" I turn back to the rest of the room. "Great job today, everyone. Remember to practice these inversions everyday. They will help you look and feel better than any plastic surgery or drugs can. Alright, enjoy your lunch!" Lily and I are swarmed by people at the end of the class, exchanging hugs with group members as they praise Lily for her maturity and say how impressed they are with this nine-year old is running the class.

I look past everyone and see Sarah and Luke towards the back. "You know where I'll be!" Sarah yells. She's so beautiful with her hand on her belly, and her long dark hair draping her shoulder in a loose braid. She's due in a few weeks. These days she and Luke rush straight to the Nourish Room after yoga, and then she goes to one of the hammocks outside to take a nap. I remember those days when I was pregnant. I took so many naps and ate every hour or so. I feel a sting in my chest as I remember the days and weeks after I gave birth. I couldn't even enjoy each sweet moment because I was a sleep-deprived, burnt-out wreck, so stressed from having to go back to work full-time after only six weeks of maternity leave. That seems like a lifetime ago.

Luke guides Sarah out the door with his fingertips on her lower back. Helen and Kyle are their other halves. The lovebirds all wave and blow kisses to me from across the room as they exit. They know it's hit or miss if I'll meet up with them. Sometimes, or I should say most of the time, I like going on a walk by myself and taking in the peace and quiet between group activities. These days, I give myself permission to tune in and do self-care, even if it means going against the grain.

The class scatters and shuffles out one by one, carrying their rolled-up mats, some slipping on flip-flops, others staying barefoot. I shut off the sound and light system once the room has cleared out.

"Mom, can I go paddle boarding after lunch? Jake and Jane said they can take us," Lily asks from across the room. I turn around and see her sandwiched between the twins. There's not a trace of shyness in her voice.

"You can," I say. I'm still getting used to her confidence standing before me. Jake and Jane are just past them, and we send each other a thumbs-up. "I'm going for a walk and I'll be in Surfer's Garden if you need anything. And make sure you have your bag with you, because it's Dad and Emma's night tonight," I tell her. "He closes his office around five today, and Emma will pick you up from the taxi boat about a half an hour after that."

After Dylan passed the bar exam, he met Emma. I I couldn't have asked for a better stepmom for Lily. And she's a better wife for Dylan than I could have been. I think he truly heard me, and I see him being a great husband now. Emma helped him quit drinking and pull out of the depression he was in for about two years after the quake. She's wonderful with Lily, and it's the greatest gift. We haven't gotten to the point of all of us being on hanging out terms, and we might never get there. But I'm happy Dylan's smiling and taking care of himself these days. I realize that sometimes we're in each other's lives for a particular time and for a particular reason, and that it doesn't mean we're failures just because it didn't work out as we originally planned. Maybe it's exactly what the universe had planned for us all along.

Lily's bag is already on her shoulder. "Got it, Mom. Love you!" she says and disappears with the twins. I love you too, my angel, I say to her telepathically.

I grab my tote bag, which holds my water bottle and the veggie wrap I made this morning. I slide my feet into my sandals and head out of the Raw Room and along the island's pathway. I follow the sandy ground with the ocean to my right and a sea of grass to my left. I run my fingers through my chin-length hair, feeling the palm of my hand resting on the back of my neck. It's been a couple years now and I still can't believe I chopped it all off. I smile to myself.

I reach into my bag and pull out my leftovers from last night, peeling away the parchment paper to unveil my favorite lunch in the entire world: my arugula, truffle aioli, marinated tempeh burger with Swiss cheese and sliced avocado. I experimented with the aioli sauce so many times, and I'm pretty sure I've perfected it. It has a crunch and smoothness as I savor it in my mouth. Sometimes my only way to connect with the past is through my senses. And right now, I'm loving that I can taste my memories all this years ago with Natalia at Sunkissed Café.

I take in the sweet and salty flavors as I walk past the Focus Room. The muffled voice of the new intern leaks out of the room. She's finishing up one of the island's favorite groups. It's called "Run For Your Mind, Write For Your Life."

Those words are pure gold for self-care. They start with a short standing meditation to practice redirecting their attention to the breath and to state their intention for the run. Then they do a three-hour run/write marathon, where they run a mile, come back to the Focus Room and write for 45 minutes with the guided discipline of the facilitator. Then they run another mile, write some more, and repeat the cycle. Even if someone wants to run faster or slower, or write for shorter or longer, they all maintain the same pace to support one another.

A newer group we started a few weeks ago is called VRIC, *Virtual Reality for the Inner Child.* We created a Virtual Reality program where couples and families do therapy sessions in a revolutionary way. They put on VR goggles, and when they are emotionally unsettled, I ask how old they're feeling. Some may say they feel like a toddler having a tantrum, while others may identify with being an obstinate teen.

Through the artificial intelligence, they can see the other person as the age they are acting. They get to see how they've emotionally regressed, and can have empathy for the other person. Then they do their own Inner Child work by working through those core issues of self-esteem and attachment needs.

When I reach the grassy area with the wooden sign I painted with the words *Surfer's Garden*, I slip off my sandals. At the edge, near the water, racks hold surfboards and paddle-boards for anyone to borrow. A blue and green-striped hammock awaits me. I climb awkwardly into it, no matter how many times I've laid there. I feel myself floating mid-air and swinging slightly.

"Good afternoon, Jelina!" One of the island regulars waves to me as he walks by.

"Hey, Tom!" I wave back. I've gotten used to the attention by now, although I still blush from being in the spotlight. Somehow I've become a celebrity around here. I don't know how that happened. I'm still doing the same things I've always done: love my kid, run therapy groups, listen to Jack Johnson. But after the earthquake, after all that death and loss and destruction and fear, and after my divorce, came this renaissance - this rebirth of my life, of Lily's life, of so many of our lives.

Palm trees and plants surround the island. My favorites are the ones called "Yesterday, Today & Tomorrow" because of the three colors of the flowers. From spring to summer, they transform from dark purple to light purple to white. I think back to how things were so different and I never thought I'd get out of that stuck existence. And now I see that everything grows and morphs and transforms. Everything. We're all in this garden that's being planted and growing and blossoming and dying and replanted and growing. We're in this endless cycle of death from what we no longer need, and replanting anew.

I can see my art therapy work displayed on the digital screen we had installed a week ago. It alternates displaying various artwork every 30 seconds. When the earthquake happened, I didn't have time to grab a single thing. The painting I made was in a PTSD process group a friend of mine facilitated. It was of a memory that replays in my mind every single day.

The scene is a view overlooking Santa Monica Beach, with the pier and roller coaster on the left and sailboats floating along the horizon on the right, and me in the middle, sitting on the green bench, awaiting the moment I was going to see Natalia for lunch. I went through so many days of intense tears, stinging heartache. But I could always close my eyes and be right back there, 35 years old, smelling the ocean water, feeling the Santa Monica breeze, sitting at the Sunkissed Café, listening to Italian music.

I quiet my mind and I can feel Natalia's arms slowly wrapping around me like the very first time, the smell of her skin, and the sound of her saying gently, "You made it. Keep going." It's like a video clip I can replay every day. I feel a tear rolling down my cheek.

I take a deep breath, and open my eyes. Acceptance. Powerlessness. I'm so grateful to have even known a love like that. The quake may have taken her away from me, but nothing could ever take away our memories, and our soul connection.

I miss you.

Chapter Seventeen: Breathe Me

The sun is setting and Lily's standing in the shallow end of the pool with the twins, and they're all playing entertaining the younger kids. They've turned a boogie board upside down and are doing magic tricks with cups on top, giggling. She's so funny, smart, playful and outgoing, leading the other children in groups and teaching them dances. I watch her eyes follow a butterfly for a moment, and I know she's thinking of Miss Kayla. There are moments in life when we're meant to keep the cameras down, and we're meant to keep pictures in our minds. This is one of those moments.

I stand up and stroll along the path towards the water's edge. The one bench that survived the quake sits up ahead. It's the same green bench I remember sitting on when I was a little girl looking out at a much different, but similar, view. I reach it and settle in, letting its solid back hold me up.

I don't know what it is about the ocean, but it's always been a powerful and magical safe haven for me. Maybe it's the comforting quiet that comes with the rhythm of the waves crashing in the background, or that somehow just by feeling the sand beneath me and letting my eyes gaze across the water and the sky, any worry I have seems small in contrast.

I feel pure freedom in this very moment. Freedom to me means not feeling trapped, knowing our choices and feeling empowered, being able to have breathing room, not being forced to do anything I don't want to do. The more control we have over ourselves, the easier it is to let things go in our lives. The faint sound of the waves outside my window are conducting the rhythm of my breath.

I lean forward and grab the bench seat underneath me. My hand feels something smooth under my seat. *Oh my God! No way.*

I reach underneath the seat and there it is. The envelope is still stuck there. I can't believe it! Those words and thoughts survived everything! My heart is beating faster. I peel open the envelope and pull the soft paper. Tears roll down my cheeks.

October 4, 1993

Dear Big Me,

I'm scared. I'm smaller and younger than the other kids in class. Miss Vikki is nice, but she says I'm too shy. My best friend is Tina and I like her. We eat lunch together and play and write in our journals everyday. I don't like going to Daddy's. My uncle is weird. I need you to take care of me. Will I be ok? I wish I could be a grown up so I could go away and feel safe. Please take care of me and don't forget about me.

Love, Little Me

I'm no longer neglecting my inner child - myself. History doesn't have to repeat itself when we let ourselves lean into vulnerability and have the courage to change it.

I swear I can hear someone playing Jack Johnson on a guitar as I walk closer to the water. My heart skips a beat. The familiar song combined with this letter in my hands gives me goosebumps. I follow the sounds and end up at the dock. As the guitar sounds get louder, I see that it's one of the guys from my yoga class this morning. Some things have remained a consistent thread to our past, and for a moment I'm transported back to the days I'd walk right by my dad and sensed there was some kind of connection and yet had no idea at the time. Funny. Life really is a dream, isn't it? I smile to myself.

I let my flip-flops take me along the wooden beams of the dock, listening to them creak with each step. It's perfect right now. There isn't a boat moving on the water, and the waves are gently kissing the shore. I reach the edge of the dock and sit, letting my feet dangle in the cool water, as I bring my back down to lay flat, with my arms resting along my sides.

The guitar melody is now a different one. I can't quite place it, but I know this one. I feel the warm ocean air against my skin. A tear rolls down my cheek when I recognize it. The melody of "Breathe Me" continues to flow through my ears and my eyes close and I just listen. That chapter of my life, so long ago now, comes flooding back to me. Natalia and I had that magical experience in the sound bath together. It's as if I can feel her on my skin right now as I remember when her fingertips first touched mine.

"Don't neglect your happiness for anyone. You can live happier beyond your wildest dreams." Her words still move me all these years later, just like they did when she first said them to me. I slowly glide my fingertips against each other, taking her memory in. I open my eyes to look up at the calming sky.

I pull myself up to sit, with my palms behind me on the dock holding me up. I look out at the glowing water. It's more and more beautiful everyday. I close my eyes, slowing down my breath and my thoughts, letting my mouth open slightly. The warm ocean breeze grazes my tongue and every cell of my skin, and I take in the serenity of this moment.

Natalia's arms slowly wrap around me from behind like she used to do. It feels like a dream—one I've had a thousand times. My whole body softens as I smell her hair, and my neck gets chills from the tingle of her breath. I put my finger to my mouth and let it trace the outline of my lips. The swirls of excitement and anxiety are exhilarating. "Baby," her lips are near my ear and my skin feels her whisper. "*You made it. Keep going.*"

If you or someone you care about is suffering from codependency, marital or relationship issues, trauma, anxiety, depression, or
medicating feelings with drugs or alcohol, please reach out for professional help.
You're not alone, and it can get better.

In the United States:
www.psychologytoday.com
U.S. Mental Health Hotline 800-448-3000

Outside of the United States:
Search for a mental health professional in your area.

Acknowledgements

To go from "I'd like to write this story some-day" to "My book is finished" is a bit surreal. - And a novel, at that. I have some very special people I'd like to express my gratitude towards who made this book possible.

Thank you, Sabrina. You are the most incredible human I know, and I'm lucky enough to get to call you my daughter. You inspire me everyday, remind me to live in the moment, to let go of overthinking, and to lean into life whole-heartedly. I love you from the bottom of my heart.

Mom and Jim, how do I say thank you for everything? I guess just like that. And for supporting me with all the random ideas I get and for being the safety net in my life.

Jeff Blume, thank you for being the least judgmental person I've met and for your persistent encouragement, insights, and wisdom and for endlessly believing in me and my dreams.

To my dear friends who inspire me, encourage me, and accept me as I am and could see me finishing this thing long before I ever thought I would, especially
Thasja, Holly, Sunny, JACS, Jenny and Lisa.

To the editors at Kevin Anderson and Associates, thank you for helping me comb through my very rough drafts.

To my clients, I'm grateful you let me in and let me walk alongside you through your journeys.

To you, the reader. It's an honor that I can share the ideas in my mind straight to yours in this manner. Thank you for reading and listening. I hope this story inspires you to never neglect your happiness, never give up, and to do everything you can to take care of yourself and live healthier and happier beyond your wildest dreams.

Keep going,
Angela

Visit me at www.LAMindSpa.com